THE GIANT BABY

ALLAN AHLBERG

The Giant Baby

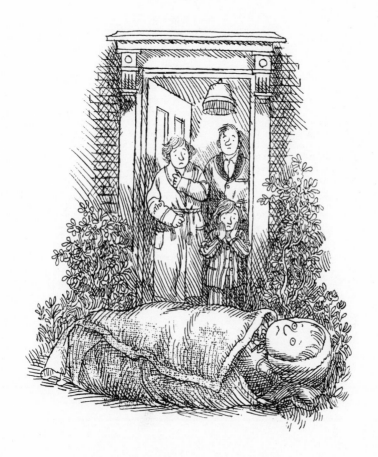

Illustrated by Fritz Wegner

VIKING

VIKING

Published by the Penguin Group
Penguin Books Ltd, 27 Wrights Lane, London w8 5TZ, England
Penguin Books USA Inc., 375 Hudson Street, New York, New York 10014, USA
Penguin Books Australia Ltd, Ringwood, Victoria, Australia
Penguin Books Canada Ltd, 10 Alcorn Avenue, Toronto, Ontario, Canada m4v 3B2
Penguin Books (NZ) Ltd, 182–190 Wairau Road, Auckland 10, New Zealand

Penguin Books Ltd, Registered Offices: Harmondsworth, Middlesex, England

First published 1994
1 3 5 7 9 10 8 6 4 2
First edition

Text copyright © Allan Ahlberg, 1994
Illustrations copyright © Fritz Wegner, 1994

Consultant Designer: Douglas Martin

Phototypesetting by Goodfellow & Egan Ltd, Cambridge

Made and printed in Great Britain by Butler & Tanner Ltd, Frome and London

A CIP catalogue record for this book is available from the British Library

ISBN 0–670–84864–6

Contents

This book derives from Allan Ahlberg's play
The Giant's Baby. Music by Colin Matthews,
directed by Vicki Ireland, first performed at the Polka Theatre,
Wimbledon, London, 20 June 1990.

I

Poor Little Thing

LONG AGO, before television, when cars were shaped like cardboard boxes and aeroplanes were made of wood, there was a girl named Alice Hicks who wanted a baby brother, although, as she said, a sister would do. Most of her friends had brothers or sisters, little or big – little *and* big. Alice herself was an only child. Her parents, however, thought differently. It was years since Alice had been a baby, but they remembered it well: the nappies, the noise; late nights and early mornings. They had no wish to go through it again. Also, there was another reason, or so they claimed: the house was too small, which it was – quite tiny, really. So her mum said, 'No room!' And her dad said, 'Have a goldfish.'

Alice didn't want a goldfish and said the baby could share her room. Her mum and dad refused to listen.

'There's hardly room to swing a cat,' said Mr Hicks.

'I don't want a cat, I want a brother.'

'Yes, and y'know what? As soon as he arrives, he'll want one.'

'Or she,' said Mrs Hicks.

'He won't want one,' Alice declared. 'He'll have me.'

Mr Hicks smiled ruefully. 'No, *we've* got you.' He lowered his voice. 'That's enough for anybody.'

'George!'

'Dad!'

'Well...' said Mr Hicks.

Soon the argument fizzled out, as it usually did. (Alice's 'baby brother campaign' had been on the go for two or three months. She wasn't getting anywhere, but neither was she giving up.) After tea, Alice played in the garden. She found a caterpillar and made a home for it in a pickle jar. She cycled round to her cousin Ethel's, but Ethel was out. Before bedtime, she had a game of Snap with her mum and dad.

'Snap!' yelled Alice.

'She's cheating,' grumbled Mr Hicks.

'No, she's not,' said Mrs Hicks, her eyes fixed firmly on the cards. 'She's just – snap! – quick.'

THAT NIGHT Alice had trouble getting to sleep. She held a conversation with her teddy under the bedclothes. (Teddy didn't know much but he was a good listener.) She picked at a skipping-accident scab on her elbow. She shuffled about in the bed . . . and hummed. Eventually, she dropped off. Then, four and a half hours later at three o'clock in the morning, she woke up again.

Feeling thirsty, Alice tiptoed down to the kitchen. She poured a glass of lemonade from a jug in the pantry and took a biscuit from the barrel. She sat at the table fiddling with the cruet. Suddenly, she raised her head. The kitchen light had begun to swing.

Boom! – there was a tremendous thud outside – and another – and another – getting louder, or nearer, or both. An extraordinary vibration rose up through the floor, cups and saucers rattled on the dresser, a distant dog began to bark. In a panic, Alice dropped her biscuit and ducked under the table. Unnoticed in the hall, the clock stopped. Then, just as suddenly, the earthquake (was it?) or thunderous footsteps (were they?) faded . . . faded . . . to silence.

Alice emerged. There was a perplexed look in her eyes and she was biting her lip. 'Mum and Dad,' she thought. 'I'll wake 'em up!' But they were awake already, roused by the rattling of the water jug, coat-hangers and suchlike in *their* room. (Some of the neighbours were awake as well.)

Alice was heading for the stairs when there was another sound, this time more . . . curious, like water gurgling down a plug-hole; like laughter, possibly. She held her breath. There it was again. It seemed to be coming through the letterbox. What could it be? Alice turned the key in the lock and opened the door.

There on the step, in the light from a street lamp, smiling and gurgling to himself, was an amazingly *large* baby.

'IT'S A . . . BABY!' Alice was mystified (of course), flabbergasted (naturally), but most of all delighted.

Mr and Mrs Hicks, when they arrived, were not delighted.

'Alice? What are you doing here?'

'What's this?'

'It's a baby, Dad – a baby!'

Mr Hicks peered suspiciously at the enormous bundle. 'Baby? That's no baby – it's bigger than me.'

'It *is* a baby, George,' said Mrs Hicks. 'Good grief!'

'Where's it come from then?' Mr Hicks stepped outside. 'Who's dumped it here?' The sky was clouded over and black; a light drizzle was falling. Mr Hicks opened the gate and looked up and down the street. But as far as he could see, which was, perhaps, not far enough, there was no one who might have lost or left such a baby.

Mrs Hicks joined him, clutching her dressing-gown to her throat. 'We'd best bring him in. It's raining.'

With much straining and heaving, Alice and her parents pushed and dragged the giant baby along the hall as though he were a sledge. The baby, by the look of him, was not distressed at being treated in this way, or bothered, come to that, to find himself abandoned. He waved his arms and took much interest in his surroundings as they slid by.

In the kitchen, Mr Hicks slumped in a chair while

Alice and her mum knelt beside the baby.

Mr Hicks looked stunned. 'What d'you make of it?'

'Beats me,' said Mrs Hicks.

'Can we keep him, Dad?'

'Perhaps it's a sort of . . .' Mrs Hicks struggled to believe what she was seeing. 'A sort of . . . I don't know.'

'A miracle!' suggested Alice. 'Like Moses in the Bulrushes. *Can* we keep him?'

Mr Hicks looked more bemused than ever. 'Keep him? Baby that size? He could keep us.'

'Must've been that noise we heard.' Mrs Hicks glanced in awe towards the ceiling. 'Giant's footsteps.'

'No – there's no such thing as,' Mr Hicks studied the stupendous baby, who was studying him, '. . . er, giants.'

And, really, that was true. For although the world was different in those days – hotter summers, warmer winters, steamier trains – it was not that different. Records were played on wind-up gramophones with horns, school desks had ink-wells in them, the rag-and-bone man roamed the streets with his horse and cart – but giants? No. They were as unlikely then as they would be now. Well, nearly.

Alice studied the baby studying her dad. He wore, the baby that is, a woolly hat with a matinée coat and matching bootees. He was wrapped in a knitted shawl from the folds of which he now produced a rattle.

'Look, Dad – he's smiling! I think he likes you.'

Mr Hicks leant forward warily.

'He's got a rattle,' said Mrs Hicks.

Mr Hicks scoffed, 'That's no rattle, it's a war club.' Whereupon – 'Aaargh!' – the baby inadvertently clubbed him with it.

Mr Hicks rubbed his head and grabbed the rattle. 'Give it here, y'brute!' But the giant baby hung on and, with his superior strength, kept possession. Mr Hicks heaved harder. At last, the baby's lip began to tremble, his face became all puckered up and, 'Waaaaa!' he cried. He didn't let go of the rattle, though.

'Dad! Now look what you've done! You've upset him – poor little thing.'

'Poor little thing? He's not a poor little thing. *I'm* a poor little thing!'

Mrs Hicks was patting the baby's back. 'Don't shout, George – there, there – you'll scare him. He's only a baby, after all.'

'And an orphan!' Alice looked accusingly at her dad. 'Isn't he, Mum? Can we keep him?'

The baby's tears subsided. Alice amused him with the tasselled cord of her mother's dressing-gown. Mr Hicks slumped back in his chair and twiddled absent-mindedly with Alice's half-eaten biscuit. Then, less absent-mindedly, he ate it.

'Anyway, what d'you think, Marion?'

'I think we should keep him,' said Alice.

'There's not a lot we can do now,' said Mrs Hicks. 'Have to wait till morning.'

Mr Hicks yawned. 'I suppose you're right. Let's sleep on it.' He got to his feet. 'Hang on, where's he going to sleep?'

'My bed!' cried Alice.

6

'Too small,' said her mum.

'All right, your bed!'

'Our bed?' Mr Hicks frowned. 'He's not having our bed. Let's put him in the wash-house.'

'George!'

'Dad!'

'Well . . .'

With much difficulty – 'You two get his feet, I'll get the rest of him!' – the giant baby was hauled up the stairs – 'It's like moving a wardrobe!' – and onto the Hickses' bed. While her parents gasped for breath, Alice rushed from the room, returning with a huge teddy.

'Look, Mum, it's that big bear from Auntie Joan.'

'Oh, yes.'

Alice held the bear out to the baby, who showed an immediate affection for it. Mrs Hicks took the opportunity to remove his hat and matinée coat. Mr Hicks rose wearily from the bed.

'George, where're you going?'

'Downstairs. I've just thought: we'll need a note for the milkman.'

Mr Hicks wrote 15 PINTS PLEASE on a postcard and left it on the step. Before closing the door, he peered, hopefully perhaps, but in trepidation too, into the night. But there was nothing to see, no giant pram or nurserymaid or mum; only the still wet and gleaming street and the dark houses.

Alice and her mum tucked the baby in.

'Look at him lying there.'

'Yes,' said Alice. '*He* doesn't know how big he is, does he?'

Mrs Hicks looked thoughtful. 'I wonder where he *has* come from. I mean, it doesn't make sense, really.'

She ushered Alice from the room and put out the light. The mysterious giant baby slept. Not long after, Alice slept too. And Alice's mum on the sofa slept. And Alice's dad in the bath more or less slept.

2

A Baby and a Half

THE NEXT MORNING, Alice was first to wake. Sunlight was slanting in through a gap in the curtains. The heavy scent of next door's Spanish vine drifted in at the open window. Pigeons were cooing on the roof, the milkman's horse neighed further up the street. For a moment Alice sat up in bed feeling oddly excited but not knowing why. Then she remembered the giant baby and rushed into her parents' room. There he lay (it was true – it had happened!), enormous, serene and, Alice wrinkled her nose . . . smelly.

There were no disposable nappies in those days, but a smelly baby was a smelly baby; some things never change. Later, it took courageous work from Mrs Hicks – and Mr Hicks, and Alice – to unpin one tremendous soggy nappy, wipe off and powder one tremendous bum and bundle it up again, this time in a bath towel. Throughout all this, the baby remained cheerful. He waved his podgy arms and kicked his podgy legs. It took all three of them to hold him down while the giant safety-pin was fixed. Mr Hicks carried the dirty nappy off, holding it out like a suspect bomb.

Breakfast followed. The giant baby sat raised up to the table on an easy chair with pillows and cushions wedged in around him. He looked bigger than ever, and

had an appetite to match. (Alice, fascinated by his capacity, kept bringing him more.) Presently, Mr Hicks arrived for *his* breakfast.

'Any toast?'

'Sorry, dear, the baby's had it all.'

'Cornflakes, then.'

'No. All gone.'

'Eggs?'

'No.'

'Bacon?'

'No.'

'Sausage?'

'No.'

Mr Hicks stared gloomily at his empty plate. Alice

was crouched behind the baby's chair playing 'Peepo!' with him. The baby, amused and *be*mused by her swift comings and goings, gesticulated with his spoon. 'Ba-ba-ba-ba!'

'Careful, Alice,' said her mum.

'Peepo!' cried Alice.

'Ba-ba-ba!'

'You'll get him all . . .'

Bang! The baby's spoon came down and shattered a cornflakes bowl.

'. . . excited.'

Mr Hicks surveyed the wreckage and rescued a couple of cornflakes.

'So,' said Mrs Hicks, 'what's next?'

Mr Hicks didn't hesitate. 'What's next? I shall phone the Town Hall as soon as they open and dispose of this hooligan.'

Mrs Hicks nodded. 'It's for the best. *Somebody'll* claim him.'

'No, they won't,' said Alice. 'He'll get put in a home, I'll bet! We should keep him.'

'Oh, Alice – we can't keep him.'

'He's too big,' said Mr Hicks.

'Anyway, he's not ours.' Mrs Hicks gave Alice a quick cuddle. 'He's got his own family . . . somewhere.'

Alice said nothing. She brushed a tear from her eye and scowled.

Meanwhile, a scowl or something like it was gathering on the baby's face. His cheeks were getting redder and filling out.

Alice was the first to notice. 'Look at him – something's wrong!'

The baby's cheeks continued to bulge; an expression of concentration showed in his eyes. For a moment there was silence. Then, 'Burp!' the baby exploded.

Mrs Hicks patted his back. 'It's all right, he's full of wind.'

'He's full of breakfast,' said Mr Hicks.

AT NINE O'CLOCK Mr Hicks phoned the Town Hall. Alice positioned herself on the landing and eavesdropped. From time to time she added her own whispered commentary to the things her dad was saying: 'A large abandoned baby . . . (we found him) . . . middle of the night . . . (he's ours) . . . doorstep . . . (we should keep him) . . .' and so on.

Mr Hicks was out of luck. The problem was, it was Saturday and most of the Town Hall was shut. Those departments that were open assumed he was exaggerating the baby's size and asked him to phone back on Monday. It was only a baby, after all; surely he could cope till then. Eventually, Mr Hicks hung up the phone and sat at the foot of the stairs. Mrs Hicks – she had been eavesdropping in the kitchen – joined him.

'Cheer up, George, it won't be for long.'

'I could always phone the police,' said Mr Hicks, tentatively.

'No.' Mrs Hicks took his arm and pulled him to his feet. 'You can come shopping with me instead.'

'Shopping? What for?'

'Baby things. We'll go and Alice can mind the baby.'

Whereupon, a suddenly cheerful Alice – 'I could take him in the garden!' – came hurtling down the stairs.

'Good idea,' said Mr Hicks. 'You could roll the lawn with him.'

ALICE played with the baby in the garden. Her amazement at his size and bewilderment concerning his arrival were already fading. Familiarity was taking their place. All the same, when the giant baby showed his preference for real rather than toy bricks, or smashed the occasional flower pot with his rattle, even Alice could sense the mystery of him. Otherwise, all seemed normal. He was a baby, which was what she wanted him to be, and much in need of entertainment, which she was happy to provide. As for the baby, surrounded by these miniature people with their miniature possessions, he could've been hugely amazed. There again, who knows? With babies it is hard to tell.

Alice carried out onto the grass a supply of toys, some dating back to when she was a baby, and household items; the colander was especially popular. Warm May sunshine filled the garden, the beginning of one of those normal or remarkable summers I mentioned earlier. In the sky a silver airship with an advertisement for 'MARMITE' moved steadily towards the horizon. A wobbly, ever-deepening voice from a wind-up gramophone winding down in someone's garden came drifting over the hedge.

Alice was preparing to play 'Peepo!' with the baby. (He had just casually tossed a toy giraffe onto the roof.)

She took a sheet, threw it over him, pulled it off. 'Peepo!' The baby loved it. His looks and gestures said, 'Again!' Alice covered him up once more.

At that moment the postman arrived. 'Hallo, there! Couple of letters for you.'

'Hallo,' said Alice, her attention on the baby, and she pulled the sheet. 'Peepo!'

The postman stared, as though Alice had performed a conjuring trick. 'Stone the crows – he's a big 'un. What're you feeding him on?'

'Toast,' said Alice. 'Cornflakes, eggs, sausage . . .'

'I can believe it.' The postman scratched his head. 'He's a baby and a half, he is. Yes, you're a baby and a half, aren't you?'

Later, when the postman had left and the game of 'Peepo!' had become a game of 'Boo!', other visitors arrived: Auntie Joan and Cousin Horace.

'Hallo, Alice,' said her auntie. 'Playing shops?'

'No – minding the baby.' Once more she removed the sheet. 'Boo!'

'Ba-ba-ba!'

'Goodness me!' Auntie Joan dropped her bag, and even Horace, a generally unshockable boy, looked startled. '*That's* a baby? Whose is he?'

'Ours, sort of. We found him on the doorstep.'

'Really?' Auntie Joan stepped nearer. 'How amazing. Where's your mum and dad?'

'Gone shopping.' Alice replaced the sheet. 'For baby things.'

'Hmm.' Auntie Joan was relaxing now. 'I can believe it. He's a baby and a half.'

'Boo!' cried Alice.

'A baby and a half . . . Yes, a little whopper, aren't you? A little whopper.'

Auntie Joan and Horace left, promising to return. Horace on his way out whispered, 'Swop you!', meaning he'd swop with Alice for the baby. Horace was famous for swopping; he'd swop anything. In this case what he'd swop – a train set, perhaps, or a younger sister even – was not revealed.

TOWARDS LUNCHTIME Mr and Mrs Hicks returned. Mr Hicks was so piled up with shopping he had to be guided into the house. Alice rushed in and began unwrapping things.

'Did you get the rusks, Dad? Did you get the cod liver oil and malt?'

Mr Hicks had collapsed in a chair. 'I expect so; there's

everything here. Anybody wants shopping now, they'll have to come to us.'

Alice continued her attack on the parcels. From one she removed what looked like an enormous Babygro, which was odd because the Babygro hadn't been invented yet. She held it against herself and did a little dance.

Mrs Hicks smiled. 'It was y'dad's idea.'

What Alice had was the largest available pair of 'coms', a popular form of gentlemen's underwear in those days. (Now there's a curious thing: the first Babygros in all the world and it was the men wearing them!)

Mrs Hicks stepped out into the garden and knelt beside the baby. 'He looks peaceful.'

Alice joined her, talking excitedly about the visitors – 'Horace wanted to swop!' – and pointing out the forlorn giraffe in the guttering. At this point the final visitor of the morning came bounding up the path. It was a reporter from the local paper. News of the giant baby had spread; news of this kind usually does.

The reporter was young, enthusiastic and quick. He asked questions, made notes, drank tea and took photographs, all in the space of ten minutes.

'Smile, please! That's . . . beautiful. Just the ticket. Right, I'm off!'

While the reporter was packing his camera, Mr Hicks hung around. 'When will it be in the paper?'

'Later today,' said the reporter, now bounding down the path. 'This is big news – front page! Bye!'

Mr Hicks rubbed his hands and strutted a little. 'Front page! Did you hear that?'

'Hmm.' Mrs Hicks and Alice were trying to measure the Babygro against the baby.

'I always wanted to be in the papers,' said Mr Hicks.

'You could be famous, Dad!'

'Oh, I don't know.' Mr Hicks looked pleased.

'Ba-ba-ba!'

'He's hungry, I'll bet,' Mrs Hicks said.

'Watch this, Mum!' Alice tossed the sheet over the baby.

'Just think,' said Mr Hicks. 'I was a baby once . . . Amazing.'

'Boo!' cried Alice.

Suddenly, coincidentally, the three of them were struck anew by the *strangeness* of recent events. An expression of bewilderment appeared to pass from one face to the other. Then it was gone. Mrs Hicks swopped the baby's hat for a gentleman's sun hat she had bought. The sun itself shone down from a cloudless sky in which a tiny biplane had replaced the airship. A clear unwavering voice from a wind-up gramophone came drifting over the hedge.

3

Horace

AFTER LUNCH, Alice shelled a few peas with her dad, then wandered off to play in her room. (The giant baby, following a burst of 'mysterious' bawling, had dozed off in his chair and was not to be disturbed.)

At half-past two there was a knock at the door – 'Yoo-hoo!' – and in walked Auntie Joan and Horace. They had come to see the baby again and hear more about him. But there was another purpose to the visit. Auntie Joan had with her, parked outside, a pram! Borrowed, it seemed, from her neighbour, Mrs Bissell; been in the wash-house for a while, so in need of a wipe; Mrs Bissell's twins grown out of it now; Mrs Bissell still having trouble with her legs, poor soul . . . and so on.

Oh, and one other thing: 'It was all Horace's idea,' said Auntie Joan. 'Wasn't it, pet?'

Horace nodded.

'He went round to Mrs Bissell's and everything. Didn't you, love?'

Horace grunted.

'He's a softy, really.' Auntie Joan gave him a squeeze. He put up with it for a moment, then slid sideways from her grasp.

Alice missed some of this, having rushed outside at

the first mention of a pram. On her return, she eyed
Horace suspiciously. He was not noted for his good
deeds or fondness for babies. Horace stood his ground
and eyed her back. Actually, I should say he *one*-eyed
her back. Horace had trouble with his eyesight and wore
glasses with black tape over one of the lenses. It gave
him the look of a small short-trousered pirate, which in
many ways he was.

The giant baby, now wide awake, was admired and
marvelled at, discussed and petted, especially by Auntie
Joan. She took an interest in the quality of knitting that
had gone into his matinée coat. By and by, the pram was
given a wipe, a clean blanket and a fresh pillow. The
baby was carried out and heaved into it. It was a
squeeze, but in he went. (Prams were big in those days,
like miniature coaches some of them, and this one was
for twins.)

Now Horace made his move. He sidled up to his
mother and whispered in her ear. She nodded. 'I don't
see why not. It's all right if they take him for a walk,
isn't it?'

Mr Hicks was eating a rusk and staring glumly at the
pram. 'Will they bring him back?'

'Of course!' Auntie Joan laughed.

Mrs Hicks gave her husband a warning look. 'Yes, all
right – just round the block.'

Alice was undecided. She wanted the pram, she
wanted the walk, but not with Horace. However, there
was little choice and anyway it might take two of them
to push it.

Off they went. Alice kept a firm grip of the pram and

a wary eye on Horace. He, for his part, asked lots of questions: had they really found the baby on the doorstep, did Alice think they'd keep him, and so on. He did his share of pushing and generally behaved himself. From time to time people in the street expressed astonishment and disbelief when confronted by the baby. Even tucked up and partially hidden in his pram, he was a perplexing sight.

'If you ask me,' said Horace, 'it's like "Strange But True", this is.'

'That's what I thought.'

'Strange But True' was a regular feature in the local paper, the only bit that Alice read. It had stories about six-legged sheep, for instance, or talking wombats.

'Do you remember them sheep?' said Horace.

'Yes, and that talking thingummy.'

'Wombat,' Horace said.

As they approached the High Street, Horace's manner changed. He stopped the pram. 'Here – get the hoods

up!' He pulled one up and started on the other.

'What are you doing?'

'Spread the blanket over!'

'What for?'

Round the corner came the reason for Horace's activity. It was his sister, Ethel, closely followed by a crowd of children.

Horace stepped between them and the pram. 'Stop there!' By now he had completed the arrangement of the blanket so that it hid the baby. 'Make a queue!'

Alice watched uneasily. 'What's going on?'

The queue, despite much pushing and complaining, began to form. 'OK.' Horace took a position beside the pram. 'Here we go: penny a peep!'

So that was it; Alice might have guessed. Horace, you see, was money mad; forever selling things at school, or doing jobs for people that, until he came along, they hardly realized were there to do.

At the mention of money the queue protested.

'How much – a penny?'

'You only said to be here for a big surprise.'

'See something big!'

'You never said we'd have to pay!'

'Shut up!' said Horace. 'I'll make it tuppence, if you like.'

But now Alice's confusion had cleared. 'No! Not tuppence, threepence or anything! He's not a side-show.'

Horace, observing her fierce expression, attempted to bargain. 'I'll split it with you.'

'No!'

Meanwhile, the queue was getting more disorderly.

'I ain't payin'.'

'Nor me.'

'Nor me!'

'There's nothing in there, anyway.'

'It's all a trick, I'll bet!'

Right on time, a giant chubby hand appeared at the edge of the blanket. (If you ask me, the baby had got tired of waiting for someone to say 'Boo!') The children gasped. The hand pulled on the blanket, the blanket fell and a giant jolly face was there for all to see . . . free.

'Cor, look at him!'

'Y' sausage!'

'Cripes!'

The crowd pushed closer. Some complained they couldn't see. Others were tempted to touch the baby, prod him even, to see if he was real. Alice was concerned at first, though she needn't have been. Horace, his money-making scheme in ruins, sulked at the back.

The children continued to admire the baby and he them.

'You know what I think,' said one. 'It's like "Strange But True".'

And others agreed.

'Yes!'

'It's like "Very Strange But True".'

'"Unbelievable But Believable"!'

'Like that giant they found in Russia.'

'Frozen stiff!'

And disagreed.

'It was a mammoth!'

And argued.

'A giant!'

'A mammoth!'

'It was a panda, I heard.'

While this was going on, a tiny girl wriggled her way to the front and held out the remains of a toffee apple to the baby. He took it, waved it, accidentally hit somebody with it and . . . ate it, stick and all.

'Crumbs!'

'Look at that!'

'Stick and all!'

There was an immediate mass search for more food. Children who lived nearby rushed into their houses. Children with money rushed into Millwood's Bread Shop. In no time a feast of iced buns and bananas, cold sausage and carrot cake, arrowroot biscuits, sherbet dip and much else besides was set before the giant baby. Under Alice's supervision and the children's fascinated gaze, he proceeded to eat the lot.

As the final bun was disappearing, Mr Hicks arrived on his way to the newsagent's. He didn't stop long or say much, but it prompted Alice to take the baby home.

The children were disappointed.

'Don't go!'

'Let's see what else he'll eat!'

'I've got a pork pie!'

But Alice had made up her mind. 'Come on, Horace.'

Reluctantly, Horace came forward. He had been trying to swop some cigarette cards for a small boy's Yo-Yo.

The children followed the pram as it began to move.

'Let me have a go,' said one.

'No, me!'

'Me!'

Horace at once perked up. A crafty smile suffused his face. 'Right-o,' he said and stopped the pram. 'Penny a push!'

4
Big Money

THE NEXT DAY was Sunday, the 'day of rest'. For Mr and Mrs Hicks, however, there was little rest to be had. The previous evening they had made a bed for the baby (a borrowed mattress on the floor) in the front room. This saved heaving him up and down the stairs. But it still left all the usual jobs, especially getting up in the night and the never-ending piles of washing. By eleven o'clock Mr Hicks was slumped in a deckchair, chewing his unlit pipe and looking forward to Monday. The baby was asleep on the grass beside him. Alice was reading a comic.

'Dad? Is it right, what Mum says: Auntie Joan was measuring the baby?'

'Yes, she's going to knit him a coat. Have to get a move on – he's leaving Monday.'

'She could send it on.' Alice appeared unconcerned.

'That's true.'

'To the *orphanage!*'

Alice, you will note, was back on the baby campaign. She had wanted a brother, now she had one. She wouldn't give him up without a fight.

After lunch Mrs Hicks had an idea. She attached a hose pipe to the kitchen tap, undressed the baby and hosed him down. The baby loved it. He squealed and waved his arms. Alice hurried into her swimming costume and joined him on the grass.

'Ba-ba-ba!'

'Shoot it in the air, Mum – like rain!'

'Ba!'

Mr Hicks looked on approvingly. It occurred to him there'd be no bath-time tonight. Last night he'd ended up wetter than anyone.

Alice, spotting his smile through the spray, tried her luck. 'It's good, isn't it? *Can* we keep him?'

'Very good,' said Mr Hicks. 'No.'

ON MONDAY MORNING at seven o'clock the phone rang; Alice answered it. It was the reporter from the local paper wanting another interview. At twenty-past seven it rang again, this time a reporter from a national paper. By eight o'clock, three other reporters had phoned and a woman from the BBC.

During this time the giant baby had yelled for his breakfast, had his nappy changed, been heaved into his chair and eaten his breakfast. He had also discovered the game of dropping spoons on the floor. Alice (principal retriever) was supposed to be getting ready for school.

'Come on, get a move on,' said her mum.

'Do I have to?'

'Yes.'

All the while the phone kept ringing, and the doorbell too. There were friends of Alice's calling for her and peering nosily round the door. Other children that she barely knew also called; two were from another school! Suddenly, there was a BBC van in the street and a radio reporter at the door. Alice let him in, although from his manner he would have come in anyway. He had a microphone in his hand with a cable leading back to the van.

'Where's the baby?'

'In the kitchen,' Alice said.

Soon the reporter was set up in the kitchen, making a nuisance of himself. Mr Hicks was keen to phone the Town Hall, if the phone ever stopped ringing. Mrs Hicks was trying to get Alice off to school. Alice was intent on staying where she was. The baby, however, wasn't busy at all.

'Will he say a few words?'

'Doubt it,' said Mr Hicks. 'He might say the same word a few times.'

'Ba-ba-ba-ba!' cried the baby.

'There you are.'

'That's *very* good!' The reporter approached the baby. 'Now, if we could just . . .' He held out the microphone. Delightedly, the baby grabbed it. (Microphones looked a bit like rattles in those days.)

'Hey – he's got the mike!'

'So he has,' said Mr Hicks.

'Let go!' The reporter pulled on the cable. 'He won't let go!'

'No, you're right.'

Desperately, the reporter heaved; effortlessly, the baby hung on. 'This is hopeless. What shall I do?'

Mr Hicks looked thoughtful. 'You could fight him for it.'

Having briefly sucked the microphone, the baby gave a yell of satisfaction and banged it on the table. This had the effect of smashing a butter dish and deafening the poor sound engineer out in the van. Eventually, the giant baby was persuaded to give up his treasure. Mrs Hicks tempted him with a rolling pin and instantly regretted it. How were they going to get *that* off him?

The reporter slumped in a chair and dropped hints about 'a nice cup of tea', which he didn't get. Shortly after, he left, trailing his cable behind him. His place was taken by another reporter. And the phone rang. Neighbours called offering help or asking to borrow a cup of sugar. And the phone rang. A door-to-door salesman called selling Kleeneze brushes. He didn't know about the giant baby, though; his visit was a coincidence. And the phone rang.

Yes, Monday was a crazy day in the Hickses' household. Alice never did go to school and her parents hardly noticed. In the afternoon, Mr Hicks got through to the Town Hall, only to encounter a particularly fussy clerk in the welfare department. She talked about special procedures and irregularities. She wanted to know the exact dimensions of the baby and the precise time of his arrival, not to mention Mr Hicks's full name, occupation and date of birth. She managed to imply that somehow he was making a nuisance of himself.

Mr Hicks kept his temper. At last, the clerk agreed that some action was necessary. An appointment was made for the welfare visitor to call, but not before Wednesday.

'*Wednesday*?' Mr Hicks turned to his wife. 'What are we supposed to do till Wednesday?'

ON TUESDAY MORNING Alice failed to go to school again, Mr Hicks failed to go to work (he was an inspector on the trams) and Mrs Hicks had the offer of a job (she was a supply teacher) but couldn't take it. The crowd in the street, large on Monday, was huge on Tuesday. People had come from miles around for a glimpse of the giant baby. There were prams and pushchairs, ponies and traps, bicycles and motor-cars. There were milkmen, breadmen, rag-and-bone men and window-cleaners. There were a great many children, most of whom, like Alice, should have been in school.

Alice was worried about Wednesday and the welfare visitor. She could see it all: the visitor would come and the baby would go. She could imagine the orphanage, too: bleak, bare and smelling of carbolic soap. Across the room, Mr Hicks was snoozing on the sofa. Alice sighed and prepared for another go at him. The doorbell rang.

When Alice opened the door, she found an unusual man smiling at her. He had bushy eyebrows and a waxed moustache. He wore a black top hat and cloak, black trousers with red stripes down the sides, a red waistcoat and white gloves. He carried a cane.

'Grubbling,' said the man and raised his hat. 'May I come in?'

Alice, dazzled by the smile that didn't falter even when the man was speaking, stepped aside.

Mr Grubbling handed a card with his name on it to Mrs Hicks. 'Basil Grubbling. Grubbling Brothers' Circus.'

'Marion Hicks.'

'George Hicks.'

'Alice!' replied the Hickses.

'And . . . *baby*,' said Mr Grubbling. He smoothed his moustache and smiled even more ('Like a piano,' thought Alice).

The baby was lolling in a sleepy way on the rug, clutching his teddy.

Mr Grubbling came straight to the point. 'I want this baby in my circus and I'll pay big money to get him.'

'No,' said Mrs Hicks.

'I mean it.' He removed a wad of money mysteriously from his cloak ('Like a conjuror,' thought Alice). '*Big* money!'

'You heard,' said Mr Hicks. 'No!'

'That's right,' said Alice. 'Clear off!'

Mr Grubbling was not dismayed. 'No deal?' Then, flourishing an even bigger wad, 'How about *very* big money?'

'No!'

'Not for any money!'

'He's just a baby.'

'Is that so?' Mr Grubbling leant on his cane. 'And what happens when he grows up? He'll go straight through the roof. I tell you, this baby belongs in the Big Top –'

'No!' cried Alice.

'– working for me –'

'No!' cried Mrs Hicks.

'– for *big* money!'

Mr Hicks laid a restraining hand on Mr Grubbling's shoulder. 'That'll do. Come on – out! Before we set the baby on you.'

Mr Grubbling held up his hands in mock surrender – 'I'll go!' – and headed for the door. 'But I'll be back. *Big* money.'

Alice rushed to the window. The crowd in the street parted in an admiring, star-struck way to let him pass. 'Do you think he will come back?'

'I doubt it,' said her mum. 'I wonder what his brother's like?'

Mr Hicks was thinking, or pretending to think, about

the money. 'How much was in that bundle, would you say?'

'Don't know – don't care!' cried Alice.

'We slipped up there; could've made our fortunes.' (Actually, the truth is they couldn't have made their fortunes since the total amount in both bundles was only two pounds, the top two; the rest was stage money.)

AFTER LUNCH Alice went unwillingly to school. Half a day was better than nothing, her parents said, the baby would be safe with them, and, that's it – no more arguing – go!

Despite her reluctance, Alice enjoyed herself. When she arrived, everyone made a huge fuss of her. As soon as the class had settled down, the teacher, in Alice's honour, told them about Romulus and Remus, the babies left on a *wolf's* doorstep, who eventually founded the famous city of Rome. He also read a chapter of *Gulliver's Travels*, the part where Gulliver was captured and tied down by the Lilliputians. This interested Alice greatly. It helped her to see things better from the baby's point of view, and made her wonder, well, what *would* happen when he grew up.

During afternoon play, Alice was the centre of a noisy discussion with as many children as could get a word in. Here's a sample:

'My dad says there's no such thing as giants.'

'What about dinosaurs then?'

'What about "King Kong"?' (*King Kong*, a film about a giant gorilla, was all the rage then.)

32

'Yeah, I saw that.'
'Hey, what if the baby gets that big!'
'And climbs the Town Hall!'
'Swatting aeroplanes!'
'In his nappy!'

'My dad says there's no such thing as King Kong.'
'Your dad's a twerp.'
'Yes,' (this was Horace), 'her *baby* could fight your dad.'

At the end of the day, Alice walked home with Ethel, Horace and about a hundred other children. Girls she hardly knew were inviting her to play at their house. Fourth-years wanted her autograph. Alice's best friend, by the way, was on holiday.

In Bridge Street a large poster for 'The Grubbling

Brothers' Circus' prompted Alice to tell Ethel about Mr Grubbling. Horace overheard and seized at once on the essential detail. 'How much was he going to pay?'

A crush of children gathered at the poster. They admired its colourful artwork and ornate lettering. They interpreted (and misinterpreted) its extravagant language: The Underwater Sensations! Sword Swallower Extraordinaire! Gravity Defied! They disagreed about the relative merits of various performers: high wire was best – no, lion-taming – clowns!

Alice remained quiet. Her attention had been caught by Mr Grubbling's somewhat idealized portrait: his shoulders were wider, his gloves whiter, his eyebrows neater and his cane had a golden gleam. His smile, though, was just as she remembered: beaming, bold . . . and villainous. It was a warm afternoon; many of the children trailed coats and cardigans. Even so, Alice shivered as she set off home.

5
So What Do You Say?

THERE WERE FIVE Grubbling brothers altogether: a remarkably tall one named Hubert,
a remarkably short one named Lionel, a
supposedly strong one named Oswald, an amazingly
dim-witted one named Gus – and Basil. The brothers
owned and ran the circus, which they had inherited
from their father. They were assisted by their mother,
their sisters Queenie and Isobel, plus various uncles,
cousins and other more distant relations. As its posters
proclaimed, the Grubbling Brothers' Circus was a truly
family concern; not that much else in the posters could
be relied on.

Hubert   Lionel   Oswald   Gus   Basil   Queenie

IT WAS NOW three o'clock in the morning: Wednesday. In a caravan on the outskirts of the town, Basil Grubbling was nursing a black eye and clutching a bottle of beer. He was dishevelled, bruised and cheerful. That was the thing about Basil: he wasn't the tallest, strongest or anything like that, but he was the most optimistic. Nothing could get him down, not even a right hook from Queenie. Queenie had delivered her punch, and a kick or two to go with it, at the family conference, which had come to an unruly end an hour earlier. She was protesting, as she often did, at the unfair, *undemocratic* way the circus was run. She had never forgiven her father for handing the business on only to his sons. In her opinion it ought really to be: The Grubbling Brothers' and Sisters' Circus. Mrs Grubbling, I may add, favoured The Grubbling Mother's, Brothers' and Sisters' Circus.

The brothers were gathered in Oswald's caravan drinking beer and being silly. What they were supposed to be doing was discussing the circus's financial state. The problem was shortage of customers brought about by an absence of star attractions. You see, the Grubblings were a numerous family, but not especially talented. Hubert, for instance, could play six musical instruments, all badly. The posters announced all manner of 'daring thrills and fun', but what they said and what the audiences saw were different things. Gravity *was* defied, after a fashion; swords swallowed, sort of; but where were the Underwater Sensations? Where was the stagecoach hold-up with real live Indians? Where were the elephants? Nowhere. In any town the first-night audience was usually good. After that the word got round and it wasn't long before performers out-numbered customers.

The caravan was crowded. Fortunately, Hubert, though tall, was flexible. He could fold himself up into a space not much larger than that occupied by Lionel. Unfortunately, Lionel, being small, felt the need to assert himself. So they cancelled each other out. The silly conversation the brothers were having had degenerated from an earlier sensible one about raising money. Now it was about spending it in absurd amounts and prepos-terous ways.

Presently, Basil returned to his own scheme for reviving the family's fortunes. He slipped his empty bottle into the capacious pocket of Gus's trousers and flourished a copy of the local paper. 'This is the answer, boys. Big baby – big news – big money!'

Previously, the brothers had scorned Basil's proposal. Now, with a pint or two of beer inside them, it seemed more attractive.

Basil tossed the paper aside. 'I can see it all.' He spread his hands to indicate the banner headline: 'The Impossible Infant!'

Hubert and Oswald took up the theme:

'The Towering Toddler!'

'The Colossal Kid!'

Then Gus said, 'I agree with Lionel.' This was confus-ing since, under the beer's influence, what he actually said was, 'Iyareewlnnnl.' Not only that, Lionel hadn't said anything.

Soon, however, Basil was off again. 'This baby *belongs* in the Big Top!'

'Working for us!' cried Lionel.

'Frrrbiiimmm . . .' (for big money), concluded Gus.

There was a pause. 'How big is he exactly?' said Hubert.

'Monumental.'

'And how would we get him?'

'Easy.' Basil smoothed his moustache. 'They've got this pram. We'll just push him off in it.'

'Push him off in it?' the brothers gasped.

'That's kidnappin'!'

'We'll never get away with it.'

'End up in jail!'

But Basil was unstoppable now. Nothing could daunt him, not even the obvious fact that everyone would know they'd stolen the baby the moment he was put on show. 'It's not a problem,' he declared. 'We'll take him to another town.' And when this was poorly received: 'Another country then!'

Basil reached over and took a swig from Gus's bottle. Gus stared perplexedly at the hand where the bottle had been, till Basil replaced it.

'Anyway, there's nothing to worry about.' Basil removed an envelope from his pocket. 'We'll have this letter of permission.'

'Who wrote it?' said Hubert.

'I did. If the worst comes to the worst, we'll say we were taken in by a clever forgery.'

The brothers looked relieved.

'It's the perfect alibi,' said Basil.

The brothers looked cheerful.

'When would we . . . pinch him exactly?' Oswald

asked.

Basil consulted his watch. 'In about half an hour. And by the way, it's borrow not pinch.'

The brothers looked joyful.

'Borrow – yeah, that's it.'

'Borrow not pinch.'

'Borrow!'

'Brrrrr . . .'

Basil beamed his villainous smile upon them, dispelling any lingering wisps of doubt (or good sense). 'So what do you say?'

THE GRUBBLING BROTHERS required no ladders, crowbars or skeleton keys to break into the Hickses' house. All they needed was Oswald's strength, such as it was, Hubert's height and Lionel's diminutive size. Oswald, buttressed by Basil, took up a position below the bathroom window, which was slightly open. (It had been a warm night.) Hubert, a lightweight despite his size, climbed onto Oswald's shoulders. Lionel, refusing

any help from Basil, heaved himself onto Oswald's back, shimmied up Hubert – 'The Human Drainpipe' – and disappeared. (Gus, incidentally, was not with them. He had got as far as the High Street before falling asleep in the bread shop doorway.)

A moment later the back door opened and Lionel peered out at Basil's knee. He gave a thumbs up sign and the others followed him back into the house. What happened next was a kidnapper's dream. It went like this:

(1)   The brothers found the giant baby fast asleep in the front room.

(2)   They got him into his pram, which was parked in the hall. This miracle of baby and torch juggling was accomplished with hardly a sound. No furniture was bumped, no vases were toppled, and the baby, amazingly, slept on.

(3)   The front door was successfully opened.

(4)   Less than ten minutes after they had entered the house, the Grubbling Brothers, complete with stolen giant baby, left it. Down the garden path they went and off into the town.

ALICE sat bolt upright in bed. One second she was fast asleep, the next, wide awake. Something was wrong; she knew it. Perhaps she'd been disturbed by the crunch of gravel on the path below her window. On the other hand, it could have been intuition.

Alice put on her sandals and descended the stairs. The door to the baby's room was open. She looked inside and gasped. The front door was open. She rushed into the garden. The gate was still swinging on its hinges. She ran up the path. The street lamps had begun to go out. A faint light lit up the eastern sky. The town was silent and deserted – or was it? Alice peered into the gloom and thought she saw ... something. She set off up the street.

Of course, what Alice should have done was wake her parents. And what they would have done was call the police. What the police undoubtedly would have done was capture the kidnappers, lock them up and return the baby to his 'rightful owners'. Later on, there would have been a trial and prison sentences, with time off for good behaviour, always supposing that the Grubbling Brothers were capable of it. When they came out they would have been placed on probation for a while. Alice, however, chose to set off up the street, so none of this occurred; well, most of it didn't.

The Grubbling Brothers were congratulating each other on their incredible skill and daring. Basil pushed the pram, with Hubert loping easily beside him. Oswald was in the rear; Lionel, his little legs a blur, determinedly in front. The giant baby was awake now, sitting up and gazing out at the emerging town. The horizon was getting lighter all the time; a last sprinkle of stars was fading in the west. The baby craned his neck, perhaps to admire the wide mysterious sky. There again, maybe he was looking for somebody.

In the High Street the brothers paused to rouse Gus from his slumbers. After a shaking, and a squirt from Lionel's trick buttonhole, they persuaded him to come along with them. Alice was close enough now to recognize Basil – 'So he did come back!' – and guess who his companions were. She dodged in doorways and kept to the shadows. Soon she was picking up snatches of conversation. Basil and the others were boasting to Gus about the break-in. They called on him to admire the latest star attraction: 'The Biggest Baby in the Universe!' Only Hubert showed any decency. He tucked the baby's blanket in and handed him a carrot. Hubert had a fondness for carrots.

In Bridge Street the brothers stopped to admire their own poster. Ten minutes later they arrived at Cummings Fields where the circus was camped. Alice got as close as she dared and hid behind a generator. The circus was silent, except for the snuffling of horses, the occasional bark of a seal. There was a smell of straw and diesel fumes. Already Alice's sandals were soaked in the dew. The early morning breeze ruffled her hair. The Town Hall clock struck five.

The Grubbling Brothers were perplexed. Having kid-napped the baby, they now had the problem of what to do with him. Not only that, they were worn out. Luckily, the giant baby was also sleepy. He slumped back in his pram and sucked his carrot.

By and by Oswald muttered something and stumbled off to his caravan. Lionel and Gus went off to theirs. Hubert raised a tent flap and Basil pushed the pram inside. Alice looked rapidly about. The tents, caravans and trailers showed no signs of life. Cables and lengths of rope cluttered the ground. A cow was staring at her over a hedge. Alice scuttled forward. Ignoring the wet grass, she wriggled under the stiff and scratchy canvas and into the tent.

Alice crouched behind a bale of hay. There was a powerful smell of horses and horse-feed. As her eyes became accustomed to the gloom, she noticed a row of stalls on the far side with ponies in them. Basil and Hubert were beside the pram. Hubert said, 'I wonder where he *has* come from?' Shortly after, Basil left the tent.

Hubert gazed into the pram. He recovered the baby's carrot (most of it), wiped it on his sleeve and ate it. He spread a horse blanket as an extra cover over the baby. He found one for himself, curled up in the straw and sank into an instant sleep.

Alice waited. The ponies snuffled in their stalls. A train whistle blew from miles away. Hubert groaned in his sleep.

Stealthily Alice emerged and approached the pram. The baby was barely visible beneath his blankets. His eyes were shut. Alice's heart was thumping. She grasped the handle and began to push. Because of the uneven

ground, it was harder work than ever. Alice flinched with every squeak of the pram's springs. At any moment she expected Hubert to leap up and grab her.

The sun was up as Alice manoeuvred the pram outside. A dazzling light lay on the fields. She paused and squinted. Wisps of smoke were rising from one of the caravans. At the window of another, a little dog in a ruff was calmly watching her.

IT WAS FIVE-THIRTY. Alice was in Bridge Street again, heading for home. A solitary cyclist went by and wobbled. He was startled to see a girl out walking the baby (any baby), and in her pyjamas, at such an hour. Alice, of course, was in a state of wild excitement. She had done it! Rescued the giant baby from a den of thieves! Wait till she told her mum and dad! Already she was picturing the scene. There would be celebrations and a party, perhaps: the giant baby in a paper hat. Alice craned forward to catch a glimpse of him. Suddenly, calamitously, a wave of panic hit her as she remembered what day it was: Wednesday! The welfare visitor – the orphanage – oh, no!

Alice sat on the wall that fronted the tram depot. A fragrant breeze, sweet pea and honeysuckle mainly, blew towards her from the allotments across the street. She was near to tears and desperate. What could she do? Who could she turn to? Had she run all those risks and rescued the giant baby only to lose him again – to an orphanage? Alice clenched her fists and frowned.

She stared across at the allotments. It was like a little town, really: little sheds and garden plots, picket fences,

verandahs even. Her grandad had his allotment in there, over the back, towards the park. Alice sometimes used to accompany him, carry his flask and sandwiches, do a bit of digging. Not lately, though; not with his poorly leg and everything. Her grandma said . . . Alice's train of thought raced on ahead. Presently, she stood up and pushed the pram across the street. She entered the allotments and made her way down various paths to her grandad's plot. She took the shed key from its secret place and opened the door. She wheeled a wheelbarrow out and the pram in.

Alice studied the baby's sleeping form. She rearranged his blankets, including the now technically stolen horse blanket. She bit her lip, hesitated, left the shed, returned, studied the baby again, left again, locked the door . . . and with a light and heavy heart ran off up the path.

6
Complications

ALICE LAY IN BED with the covers clutched to her chin. She was hot and horribly anxious. Her main concern was the baby. What if he woke up and started crying? What if somebody heard him – or didn't hear him? What if he fell out of his pram? She was worried, too, about her parents. Alice had hidden her sandals in the wardrobe, but there were angry marks on her feet where the sandals had chafed, and scratches on her arms and shoulders from wriggling under the tent. Her mum, especially, had an eagle eye.

At six-thirty the alarm went off. Alice heard her dad descend the stairs and his startled cry: 'What's this?' She heard his footsteps on the path, the gate swing and slam. She heard her mum getting up and soon *her* startled cry: 'Where is he?'

Alice's heart was thumping again, this time with embarrassment. Any minute now her parents would rush in and tell her what had happened. She'd have to pretend she didn't know; worse than that, tell *lies* to both of them.

Somehow she got away with it. First of all, it was her less-observant dad who 'woke' her. 'Alice – get dressed!' He was tucking his shirt in. 'Hurry!'

Alice feigned a yawn. 'What time is it?'

'Time to get up – come on!'

Alice leapt out of bed, got dressed and stepped on to the landing. Downstairs she could hear her mum on the phone.

'Yes, sergeant. Yes. A large baby . . . I don't know. He's gone! Yes.' Mrs Hicks fumbled with a handkerchief.

Mr Hicks shouted from the kitchen. 'Tell them the door was open!'

'The door was open,' said Mrs Hicks.

'And his pram's gone!'

'And his pram has gone . . .' Mrs Hicks sighed deeply. 'Yes . . . 42 Tucker Street.' Finally, she put the phone down and looked up the stairs, straight at Alice.

Alice felt obliged to speak – and lie. 'What's wrong, Mum?'

'Oh, Alice!'

MRS HICKS explained what had happened. To cover her confusion, Alice hurried into the baby's room. When the open bathroom window was mentioned, she ran upstairs. In one sense, though, her play-acting wasn't difficult. After all, she was almost as worried about the baby as they were. She was desperate to get back to the allotments, or at least away from the house. You see, there was something else; Alice had had a brain-wave: Horace!

While they waited for the police, Mr and Mrs Hicks searched the neighbours' gardens. Alice seized her chance, opened the gate and ran off up the street. 'I'll take a look around!' She was gone before they could stop her.

'Not too far, though!'

'Come straight back!'

Dejectedly, Mr Hicks raised the lid of a dustbin, just for something to do. Mrs Hicks had a thoughtful expression. 'Alice smells of *straw*.' Yes, she had an eagle eye all right, and an eagle nose to go with it.

ALICE was hot and gasping, but she had found Horace. He was engaged in his morning job helping the milkman. When she caught up with him, he was half-way down the vicarage path.

At first all Alice could manage to say was, 'Horace!', which he was disinclined to take notice of. He had a job to do; money to earn. Eventually, Alice got her breath back. She told Horace about the kidnapping, the rescue and the allotment shed. She told him about the welfare visitor, the orphanage, her mum and dad, and the police. Horace listened, his one visible eye wide with surprise. There were questions he would have asked, but, unusually for him, he had trouble getting a word in. His early suspicion that Alice was pulling his leg was swept away by her convincing behaviour.

'I've got to get back,' said Alice. 'They'll wonder where I am.'

Horace nodded.

'But somebody needs to go . . .' she lowered her voice, 'to the allotments.'

'Me,' said Horace.

Alice handed him the key.

WHEN SHE returned to the house, Alice found a police car parked in the street. In the kitchen a burly sergeant was questioning her mum and dad; a constable was taking notes.

'Here's Alice!' said her mum.

'Ah!' said the sergeant. 'The missing infant's sister.'

'No,' said Mr Hicks.

'Yes,' said Alice.

'Anyway,' the sergeant cleared his throat, 'let's get it straight. How big *is* this baby?'

'Big,' said Mr Hicks. 'As big as you.'

A look of disbelief appeared on the sergeant's face. The constable smiled over his notes.

'Do you have any evidence of that?'

'Yes,' said Mrs Hicks. 'This is his hat.'

'And that's his breakfast.' Mr Hicks gestured to the piled-up table laid ready the night before.

'And *this*,' cried Alice, waving the paper aloft, 'this is his photograph!'

The photograph clinched it. 'My word, he is a big 'un!' (The policemen, by the way, had lately returned from a crowd-control course, which accounts for their ignorance of recent events.)

The sergeant, whose name was Fagg, stepped over to the door. 'Come on, Dunkley – let's look for clues.'

It was now eight o'clock. While the police tramped round the house and garden, Alice did her best to steer clear of the real detective. Luckily, her mum was on the phone for some of the time and busy after that providing a description of the pram to Constable Dunkley. Out in the street a crowd was gathering, in hope of seeing the giant baby. The police car was an added attraction.

Alice was beside herself. She wanted to get away, but couldn't find the means to do it. She stood irresolutely in the hall. Sergeant Fagg came in and went upstairs. Mrs Hicks called out from the kitchen.

'Alice, you should go to school!'

Alice's spirits rose. Even so she risked the expected reply. 'Oh, Mum!'

Her dad appeared in the doorway. 'Do as your mum says.'

Alice scowled theatrically. At her mum's insistence, she drank a glass of milk and ate some toast. She collected her satchel.

In the hall, her mum gave her a hug. 'Don't worry – the police'll sort it out, I'm sure.'

Alice set off down the path. Her dad waved from an upstairs window, so did Constable Dunkley. As she reached the gate, she heard (and pretended not to) her mum say, 'Alice . . . where're your sandals?'

WHEN ALICE arrived at the allotment shed, the giant
baby was sitting up in his pram eating chocolate biscuits,
which Horace was handing him. On a table near the
window there was a banana skin, the peel of a pear,
two bottles of milk and a cup. There was a bacon sandwich wrapped in greaseproof paper (Horace's breakfast),
half a dozen comics, a penknife and a bottle of ginger
beer.

Anxiously, Alice approached the baby. How had his
ordeal affected him, she wondered. Not much, it seemed,
for all she saw was a dazzling smile of recognition,
darkened only by the circle of chocolate around his
mouth.

The baby's joy was unconfined. 'Doh!' he cried, and
flung his arms up high (and his biscuit higher). Alice

kissed his forehead and turned her attention to Horace. She had sought his help because there was no one else she could think of. Even so, she appreciated what he had done and was doing. He had gone up in her estimation.

Horace gestured to the table. 'I got a few things.'

'Me too.' Alice opened her satchel and took out some rusks in a paper bag, a bottle of baby's orange juice, some squashed jam tarts and a couple of sausages. She handed the baby a rusk.

Horace watched yearningly. 'I love rusks.'

She handed him one.

'So what's the plan?'

Alice shrugged and looked unhappy. There was no plan. All she could think of was keeping the baby away from the welfare visitor and out of the orphanage. 'We'll have to hide him for a while . . . somehow.'

Horace nodded. 'We can do that.' He gave the baby a sausage and watched with pleasure as it disappeared. He said, 'And the circus really did kidnap him?'

'Yes.'

'And you kidnapped him back?'

'Yes!'

'Hmm.' Horace appeared thoughtful. Alice had gone up in *his* estimation.

Alice removed the horse blanket from the pram and folded it over a chair. She hung her satchel on a hook behind the door. 'We're going to need some help.'

'Right.' Horace was standing at the window. 'We can get Ethel – and Kenny Copper – and Phippy!'

'Not Phippy,' said Alice.

A gleam appeared in Horace's eye. 'Hey, I've just

thought – we could have a password.' He clapped his hands in sudden satisfaction. 'And a secret knock!'

BACK AT THE CIRCUS, the Grubbling Brothers had discovered the giant baby's absence and were outraged.

'Just think of all the trouble we went to.'

'Then *somebody* strolls off with him.'

'Without a by-your-leave!'

'Who'd do such a thing?'

'It's a criminal disgrace!'

Basil was particularly upset. He had been boasting to Queenie about the baby's arrival when Hubert burst in with the news of his departure. Now Basil paced the sawdust ring of the Big Top with a grim frown on his face. His spirits seemed not to be lifted by the bowl of porridge he was eating. He turned to his brothers, who were sitting in a row along the wooden curve of the ring. 'Who's got him, that's what I want to know. Who's pinched our baby?'

There was silence for a moment. Gus raised his hand like a child in class. '"Borrowed",' he said, helpfully. 'You said "borrowed" not "pinched".'

7

The Motherhood Book

THE DRUM STREET allotments were a patch-
work of vegetable gardens, fruit bushes and
sheds. They covered an area of about fifteen
acres and backed onto the park from which they were
divided by a combination of hawthorn hedge and
chestnut palings. There were useful gaps. Now and then,
children crept in to continue their fishing in the brook,
which flowed from the park. In the appropriate seasons,
they sometimes came in search of raspberries or carrots.

Alice's grandad, Grandad Turner, had had his allotment plot for thirty years. It was his pride and joy. He
grew excellent potatoes, runner beans and peaches
(yes!). His shed was as much a den as a garden store. As
well as seed trays, flowerpots and so on, there were
other more domestic items: a table and chair, a paraffin
stove, a pipe-rack, assorted cutlery, a teapot and a cup
and saucer. There was a rag rug on the floor, faded
curtains at the window.

About the peaches: well, it really was hotter in those
days. The sun rose earlier and set later. There were a
couple of palm trees (no coconuts, though) in the park.
Grandad Turner's peach tree grew against the south side
of his shed and was not the only one in the allotments.
There was a lemon tree in the Town Hall gardens.

IT WAS NINE O'CLOCK. The school bell had just stopped ringing. Horace had his feet up. He was reading a comic and eating a rusk. Suddenly, his idyll was broken. 'Poo – is that him?'

'Yes – we'll have to change his nappy.'

'Ooh, y'devil!'

Alice opened the window while Horace fanned the air with his comic. Soon it was decided that he would sneak out and buy a few things. Alice used a page from her school notebook to make a list.

Horace had lots of money: pocket money, swops money, occasional church choir money and milkman money. Even so, he only agreed to spend some of it if Alice paid her share later. Horace, I may say, had other schemes in mind to cover his losses.

Horace departed, creeping round the side of the shed and heading towards the park. Alice gave the baby a drink of milk. She remained stationed near the fresh air of the open window. A bee thumped against the glass and made her jump. Alice watched the baby. In this little shed she was struck anew by just how big he was. Amazement blossomed inside her.

Alice thought of her best friend, Norah Stubbs, away on holiday, you may remember. She wished Norah was here and not Horace. Through the window, she saw an old man go by with a spade over his shoulder and a dog at his heels.

Horace returned full of his exploits as a secret shopper. He'd had fun, too, getting in and out of the allotments unobserved. 'There's a bloke out there. He never saw me, though.'

Horace removed a large sheet from a carrier bag. 'See, we can cut it up. It'll make *four* nappies.'

Alice was doubtful. (She had put bath towels on the list.) 'It's a bit thin.'

'No, it'll do.'

Only then came the tricky bit: *changing* the nappy.

They were not strong enough to get the baby out of his pram, so they left him in it. Horace held the sheet while Alice cut it with the garden shears. Horace went out to the tap and filled a watering can. He sprinkled the baby's bum: Alice wiped it with half a roll of cotton wool. Horace went mad with the baby powder.

When they had finished, the fragrant baby kicked his podgy legs so hard that the pram rocked like a ship in a storm. Alice and Horace took refuge at the head end.

Alice wrapped the dirty nappy in some old newspapers, which Grandad Turner kept for lining his seed trays. 'What do we do with this?'

Horace barely paused. 'Easy – we'll bury it.'

DURING THE MORNING, Alice and Horace amused the baby, shared the comics and kept watch out of the window. The shed was well back from the road. There was a useful screen of flowering peas opposite the door. Even so, vigilance was called for. In Horace's view, anything could happen: 'The police have got *blood*hounds, y'know.' Worse than that, there was the continuing threat from the Grubbling Brothers. Alice expressed the hope that she had seen the last of them. Horace thought differently. 'They pinched him once, they can pinch him again.'

Now this, as it happened, was Basil Grubbling's opinion. He had used the same phrase less than an hour before in order to cheer up his otherwise downhearted brothers. 'All we have to do,' Basil puffed on his cigar, 'is find him. So start looking.'

From mid-morning onwards the Grubbling Brothers searched high (Hubert) and low (Lionel) for the giant baby. They sauntered (Basil) and staggered (Oswald) about the town. They hunted here, there and everywhere, and nowhere (Gus – he was back in bed).

AT TWELVE O'CLOCK Horace went home for his dinner. (Alice usually had school dinners.) He took with him another list and promised not to be long. Alice shared Horace's bacon sandwich and bottle of ginger beer with the baby. She played 'Round and Round the Garden' with him for a time. The baby laughed so much he got the hiccups.

When Horace returned (with a sack over his shoulder), he was accompanied by Ethel, Kenny Copper and Phippy. Ethel had with her a rag doll, which she was hoping the baby would like.

With expressions of awe and amazement, the new arrivals gathered at the pram.

Horace smiled. 'It's like Baby Jesus and the Three Wise Men.'

'That makes you Joseph, then,' said Ethel.

Alice scowled when she realized who it made her. Actually, she was scowling already because of Phippy (Raymond Phipps). She had nothing against him: the problem was, wherever Phippy went, *little* Phippy was sure to follow, and he was a pest.

Horace was unpacking his sack, having successfully raided the pantry. Working at speed, however, he had not always made the most suitable choices. His haul included:

A tin of pilchards
A tin of peas
A tin of plums
A packet of custard powder
Four Oxos
A slab of butter
A bottle of Daddies sauce
Six home-made lemon curd tarts (which became five soon after)
A box of dog biscuits.

In addition, Horace had acquired a torch, a pack of cards, a game of Ludo and more comics.

Meanwhile, the giant baby was being joyful with his rag doll. Ethel and the others added their contributions to the pile. Alice repeated her kidnapping and orphanage story.

When she finished, Phippy whistled through his teeth.

Ethel said, 'Do you think they'll try again?'

'No.'

'Yes!' said Alice and Horace.

Horace spoke next: about money. In his opinion they needed a fund – 'A baby bank!' cried Ethel. Everybody would pay the same amount – 'A penny a day!' 'Tuppence!' 'A tanner!' – and Horace would take charge of it.

Naturally, this led to a debate and, eventually, a vote. It was agreed that:

(1)   The baby fund was a good idea
(2)   Tuppence a day was the most they could manage
(3)   *Alice* would take charge of it.

Horace sulked – his own pals voting against him! – but only briefly. It had long ago occurred to him that charging admission was the real way to make money in this situation.

Alice raised the subject of security. The giant baby was a secret, she said. Nobody should tell anybody. This led to the swearing of increasingly bloodthirsty oaths involving mothers, graves and sudden death. Horace explained that from now on they must only enter or leave the shed in ones or twos. Big crowds would give the game away. He had observed this technique in gangster films.

'And another thing: we need a secret knock.'

'And a password!' cried Ethel.

'I was coming to that.'

'What should it be?' said Phippy.

'Bum,' said Horace.

The others protested (and laughed). It was too rude and silly; an insult to the baby.

'I say it should be . . . Rockabye Baby,' said Alice.

And once again the vote was with her.

THE AFTERNOON wore on. The sun was high and the sky was blue. The air was still and heavy and hot. The allotments appeared deserted. Alice and Ethel took the opportunity to give the baby some fresh scenery by

wheeling his pram outside. Horace and Kenny had spread the horse blanket on the ground and were playing cards. Phippy was cleaning the shed window.

Ethel said, 'It's like Pinocchio, y'know. They kidnapped him.' *Pinocchio* was her current reading book.

Alice had wet her hankie and was wiping the baby's face. 'What worries me is, what will we do tonight?'

'That's what I've been thinking.'

'And me,' Phippy said.

Horace studied his cards. 'We'll have to sneak out. Take it in turns.'

'How?' said Alice.

'I can sneak out,' said Kenny.

'It'll be *dark*,' Ethel said.

ELSEWHERE, the search for the giant baby was continuing. Sergeant Fagg and Constable Dunkley had made a list of all the people who had visited the Hickses' house in the past few days. They proposed to interview every one of them. So far they had spoken to the postman, the window-cleaner, Auntie Joan and the Kleeneze brush salesman. Now they were on their way to talk to Basil Grubbling. Mr and Mrs Hicks were disconsolately roaming the streets. Auntie Joan and her friend Mrs Phipps were also out, combining a check of the town centre with a bit of shopping.

The Grubbling Brothers had stopped temporarily in order to prepare for the evening performance. When the police arrived, Basil offered them tea in the Big Top and expressed outrage at the news. It was monstrous that anyone should even think of stealing a baby ('Or borrowing him,' said Gus). If there was anything that he and his brothers could do to help . . . In the meantime, perhaps, Basil switched on his smile, how about some complimentary tickets for the sergeant's family?

AT HALF-PAST THREE, Alice went home, otherwise her parents would have wondered where she was. Her mum was looking strained, her dad, fidgety. He lit his pipe three or four times but failed to get it going. He kept glancing out of the window.

Alice made herself a sandwich. She tried to think of questions her mum and dad would expect her to ask. She remembered her sandals and ran upstairs to remove them from the wardrobe. When she came down, her dad said, 'What's that on your sleeve? Looks like cotton wool.' Which it was, and a clue. Alice was thankful it wasn't her mum who'd spotted it.

Alice stayed home for exactly an hour. At one point,

pretending to do some homework, she overheard her parents discussing her. Something was wrong, in Mrs Hicks's opinion, not just the baby, but she couldn't put her finger on it. In Mr Hicks's view, Alice was so upset she was suppressing her feelings, hiding things. Eventually, Alice was able to grab her cardigan (in which she had hidden things) and head for the door. She was going to the park, she said. To play with Ethel and Monica Copper.

'What about tea?' said her dad.

'I'll have it at Monica's!'

'What about a kiss?'

Alice gave him one and a hug to go with it. Then she kissed her mum (phoning again), hugged her too, and bolted.

WHEN ALICE returned to the shed, she found the boys sitting outside. Ethel was perched on an upturned box reading to them. The pram was half in and half out of the shed. The baby was asleep.

The boys all spoke at once:

'Listen to this!'

'Ethel's got this book.'

'It's called *The Motherhood Book*.'

Ethel, it seemed, had also been home and had returned with, among other things, this book. She held it
aloft. 'It's one our mother had when we were little.'

Phippy laughed. 'Little Horace.'

Horace ignored him. 'Read her that first bit.'

Ethel leafed back through the pages. 'This is what it's
got in it . . . "Contents: Expectant Motherhood, The
Cot and Other Necessaries"' (Ethel was a good reader),
'"the Nursery, Nursery Recipes –"'

'We're gonna cook him things,' said Horace.

'"– Baby's Knitted Clothes, Toys and How To Make
Them –"'

'I know how to make 'em,' said Kenny.

'It's got everything in it,' said Ethel. 'It's a good book.'

Alice said, 'I've been thinking: what if Grandad
comes?'

'He won't come,' said Ethel. 'You said so yourself.
He's got his bad leg.'

'Read some more,' said Horace.

Alice peeped in at the sleeping baby. She felt in her
pockets and handed round some broken biscuits.

'It says here,' said Ethel, '"*Bibs*: bibs should be
absorbent as well as decorative and are best backed or
padded with Turkish towelling. *Bootees –*"'

'He's got 'em.'

'He needs more!'

'"Baby's feet must be kept warm and little bootees of
Silkora should be provided."'

'Not little.'

'No!'

'It's boots more like, for him.'

Ethel ate her biscuit and turned a few pages. A butterfly zigzagged past. There was the faintest sound of traffic from the invisible road and children shouting in the park. 'Listen to this: "Everything a baby sees is wonderful to him –"'

'Except Phippy,' said Horace.

'"He finds infinite variety in exploring the world in which he lives."'

At that moment, the pram rocked on its springs and the giant baby lurched up. Instantly, his guardians gathered round, only to discover that though he may have looked like a flower (with his pink cheeks and fringe of golden hair), he smelt like a compost heap.

8

'Look Out!' Cried Horace

IT WAS TEATIME and this is what certain people (and one dog) were thinking:

Alice: The baby is still safe and not in the orphan-age.

Horace: If we charged admission, we could make more money than we spend.

Ethel: I won't tell *anybody* . . . only Monica.

The Giant Baby: (Nobody knows.)

Alice's Mum: Poor Alice; I'll just walk to the park and see how she is.

Auntie Joan: Where's the custard powder?

Little Phippy: Where's Phippy?

Queenie Grubbling: I'll brain that Basil!

Sergeant Fagg: Ransom note. (He had a bet on with Constable Dunkley that one would be received.)

People In and Around the Town: Where'd he go? (and for that matter): Where'd he come from?

Grandad Turner: (His leg feeling better.) Maybe I will take a little stroll.

Basil Grubbling: We *will* find him.

Horace's Dog: Where's Horace?

BACK at the allotments, the giant baby was sitting on the horse blanket playing with the wheel of the upturned wheelbarrow. Horace was reading *The Motherhood*

Book. Ethel had gone for her piano lesson, and Kenny to feed his rabbits.

'It says here,' said Horace, '"A baby's cot can be protected from draughts –"'

'I could do with a draught,' said Phippy.

'"– and to a certain extent from light and noise, by a pretty screen covered with cretonne."' (He was a good reader, too.)

'Read some more of the food part,' said Alice.

Horace flipped pages and adjusted his glasses. 'Hey – this bit's good! "At six months the baby should be given a boiled mutton bone –"'

'That's for teething!' cried Phippy.

'"Baby's weight",' said Horace. '"Regular weighing" . . . Hmm.'

A discussion followed on the advantages of weighing babies, the usefulness of clinics and the particular problems posed by this baby.

'We could weigh him at my dad's works,' Phippy said. 'They weigh lorries there.'

Alice and the others were beginning to take pride in the giant baby: their baby. They compared him favourably with the dimensions, weights and achievements of the average baby listed in the book.

'I think he's really clever,' said Alice. 'See how thoughtful he looks.'

'And brave,' said Phippy.

Horace closed the book and laid it down. He gave the baby's head a pat and the wheel a spin. 'I know what he is: an infant prodigy.'

KENNY returned with a jar of cod liver oil and malt; Ethel returned with Monica, Rosalind and another pram. Monica was Kenny's sister; Rosalind was Rosalind Millwood from the bread shop.

Kenny protested when he saw Monica. 'What's she doing here?'

Horace protested about Rosalind. 'And her – she's too little!'

Rosalind, who was little and only five and a half, clutched Ethel's arm and began to cry.

'No, she's not,' said Alice.

'Anyway,' said Ethel, 'wait till you see what she's got in her pram.'

'Dolls!' scoffed Phippy.

'And the rest.'

Ethel and Monica folded the hood and removed the cover to reveal a hidden hoard of *loaves and buns*, which clever little Rosalind had acquired from the bread shop. The fragrant smell of fresh bread was released into the air.

'Hmm, lovely!' said Phippy.

'Any cakes?' Horace said.

Soon a sandwich factory was established in the shed with the following choices:

Sugar

Pilchards

Sliced apple and cheese

Cod liver oil and malt

Daddies sauce.

Little Rosalind was having fun with the baby. (She had been promised she would in return for the bread.)

Rosalind was wearing a nurse's outfit. She had a toy stethoscope and was listening for the baby's giant heartbeat. Interestingly, *she* was sitting on *his* lap.

Horace, when he could eat no more, said, 'I'm off – I'll be back in a bit.' Phippy also departed. He needed to put in an appearance at home. It was seven o'clock. The shimmer of heat had disappeared from the allotments. The air was cooler and clearer. A magpie delivered its football-rattle call from a nearby tree. A cat slipped by unnoticed through the rhubarb.

Alice told Monica the kidnapping story, which she had heard already but insisted on hearing again. Ethel showed her *The Motherhood Book* ('What about *The Fatherhood Book?*' said Kenny) and read aloud a paragraph on infant diseases.

When Horace returned, he had with him a bottle of disinfectant and three boys. The girls welcomed the bottle but not the boys.

'You're telling too many people!'

'Think of all the tuppences, though,' said Horace.

'What's the password?' shouted Kenny from the shed.

Then Phippy showed up with two more boys and again the girls protested.

'You're telling *everybody*!'

'What'd you bring them for?'

'What'd you bring Monica for?' yelled Kenny.

For a time there was uproar. Gradually, however, good sense, curiosity and hunger prevailed. Horace sold sandwiches to the new arrivals, who were also allowed an awe-struck audience with the baby. The subject of secrecy was once more debated and oaths were sworn, even by little Rosalind. In the end it was decided: nobody, *nobody* would tell anybody anything ever again.

'It's a total secret!'

'Definitely!'

'Just the . . . eleven of us.'

'Twelve!'

'And *nobody* else.'

ELSEWHERE, though, if the secret wasn't spreading, suspicions were. Mrs Hicks and Mrs Copper had encountered each other in the park and were comparing notes. The police had received a phone call from Timothy White's chemist shop in the High Street. It concerned the sale of unusual quantities of cotton wool and baby powder to a boy with taped-over glasses. Constable Dunkley was investigating. The reporter from the local paper, keen on getting a scoop, was trailing Constable Dunkley. Hubert Grubbling, having lately seen some furtive-looking girls with a *closed* pram enter the allotments, was loping off to tell Basil. Finally, little Phippy, free for the moment from his mother's attention, was out on his perennial quest: searching for Phippy.

GRANDAD TURNER'S allotment shed was being transformed. Encouraged by the availability of disinfectant and urged on by *The Motherhood Book*, Alice, Ethel and Monica were cleaning everything in sight. They picked a few flowers and arranged them in a Vimto bottle on the table. They even polished the garden shears. Horace had got the paraffin stove going and was looking for something to cook. Archie – one of the new boys – was allowing Rosalind to bandage him up. The Hubble brothers – the three who'd arrived with Horace – were playing a wild game with the giant baby. This involved the baby hurling his rag doll everywhere and the brothers competing to retrieve it. Nigel, the remaining new arrival, was keeping watch.

Alice and Monica returned to the shed with further bunches of flowers. Alice was saying, 'Y'see, the trouble is, we can't leave him –'

'That's what I was thinking,' said Monica.

'– and we can't take him with us.'

'It's all right,' said Horace, 'we've got a plan. Archie's stayin' – aren't you?'

'Yes,' said Archie through the open window (and his bandages).

'How?' said Alice.

'Easy. He's told his mum he's stoppin' with his gran,

and his gran he's stoppin' with his mum. Haven't you?'

'Yes,' said Archie.

'He's got my torch and loads to eat; he can sleep in the chair and he's got that blanket. It's a piece of cake. Isn't it?'

'Yes,' said Archie.

DUSK WAS DESCENDING on the allotments and the town. A haze of purple and darkening blue thickened along the horizon. A pair of swans with heavy, beating wings flew low towards the park. In the vicinity of the shed, the competing smells of disinfectant and Horace's cooking filled the air. Children sat around on the blanket or lolled against the shed. Nigel said it was time he was going but made no move.

'It's time *you* were going,' said Monica to Rosalind.

'No,' Rosalind said.

The giant baby, still the focus of attention, was slumped in the centre of the blanket. There was a glazed look in his eyes; his thumb was in his mouth.

Suddenly, a shadow of apprehension passed across the children's faces. They raised their heads like nervous deer.

'Look out!' cried Horace. 'Somebody's coming.'

71

Somebody was. Mr and Mrs Hicks were coming for a start, and Auntie Joan and Mrs Copper. Mrs Millwood was coming, and Mr and Mrs Hubble. Constable Dunkley, the local reporter and the local reporter's girlfriend were also coming. Horace's dog was coming. A young man with a wheelbarrow was coming, but this was a coincidence; he had been swept up in the crowd. Some way to the rear and by and by, as it were, a bemused Grandad Turner was coming. Finally, triumphantly, like the last piece in a jigsaw puzzle, little Phippy was coming.

As the one crowd met the other there was a moment of guilty and astonished silence. Then . . . bedlam.

9
Home Again

B Y TEN O'CLOCK the allotments were deserted, the children were in bed, Horace's dog was tucking into a bowl of safely-returned biscuits and the Grubbling Brothers were in jail. They had been arrested earlier that evening in mid-performance by Constable Dunkley. A completely flummoxed Sergeant Fagg and his family were in the audience. Now the brothers languished in a cell below the police station. They complained about the lock on the door and the bars on the window. They protested their innocence.

'Let us out!'

'It's a criminal outrage!'

'We never borrowed no baby!'

'I've got my pigeons to feed!'

Only Basil was in the least calm. 'Steady, lads – we'll soon be out of here.'

'But how?' his brothers wanted to know.

'I mean, we *did* it.'

'There's evidence.'

'Witnesses!'

Basil was unimpressed. Guilt and evidence were mere quibbles to him. He took a cigar from his pocket and struck a match on Gus's bowler hat. 'Not witnesses,' he said, grandly, '*witness*: one small confusable child.' He puffed a smoke ring up towards the ceiling. 'I'll deal with her.'

ALICE was still awake, exhausted but too tired to sleep. Since leaving the allotments she had explained herself to her mum and dad, her grandad, her auntie, Constable Dunkley and Sergeant Fagg, and the local reporter. She had been told off for telling lies and praised for rescuing the baby. She had come home, had a bath and had her scratches soothed with Zambuc ointment. She had been kissed, cuddled and forgiven.

Downstairs Mr and Mrs Hicks were having supper.

'What a business,' said Mrs Hicks.

'Woll,' said Mr Hicks, with a mouthful of cake.

'Alice did well, though – the little madam.'

'Woll!'

'Fancy – rescuing that baby from five grown men.'

'Very grown, some of 'em,' said Mr Hicks.

'And pulling the wool over our eyes.'

'Yours mostly. I had my suspicions.'

'No, you didn't.' Mrs Hicks carried her cup to the sink. 'Let's look in on the baby.'

Together they entered his room and tiptoed up to the bed. There he lay: safe, sound and huge. His baby breath was fragrant, his baby cheeks were pink, and his baby hands were curled around Constable Dunkley's truncheon.

ON THURSDAY MORNING, the local paper carried the following headlines:

When Alice left for school, more reporters were waiting for her in the street and more still at the school gates. She was bombarded with questions:

'How ever did you manage it?'

'Weren't you scared?'

'Where do *you* think he's come from?'

'What's this about an orphanage?'

As the crowd of children grew, the reporters were bombarded with answers.

'Which one's Horace?'

'Me!'

'Me!'

'Not him!'

'He's not Horace!'

'I'm Horace!'

'Me!'

At lunchtime the reporter from the BBC strolled into

the girls' playground (boys and girls had separate playgrounds in those days). Soon he was submerged by a wave of girls willing to tell him anything he cared to know and more besides. Over the dividing wall a row of boys' heads appeared, also with plenty to say.

After school Alice rushed home. The baby was asleep when she arrived, so she joined her mum in the kitchen.

Mrs Hicks was reading the paper. 'Listen to this: "Famous Professor pooh-poohs giant baby".'

'What does he know?'

'"Professor J.B. Prewitt, interviewed in his Cambridge rooms, declared: 'This alleged baby –'"'

'What's he mean, "alleged"?'

'"'– is undeniably a hoax'".'

'The cheek!'

'"'A baby this size would require a mother as big as a house. This would be a physical impossibility. Such a lady would weigh seven or eight tons and need legs like a rhinoceros'" – fancy.'

Alice remained unimpressed. 'What's he a professor of? Not babies, I'll bet.'

When Mrs Hicks put the paper aside, Alice took it up and turned to her favourite feature: Strange But True. 'Listen to *this*: "A cabbage was grown in Colchester in 1928 that was the exact shape of Queen Victoria's head".'

'That's strange,' said Mrs Hicks.

'But true, though!'

A TOPIC of great interest at this time was 'The Trial'. Everybody was talking about it and rumours abounded.

Thus: the trial would take place tomorrow – next month – next year. Sir Sebastian somebody-or-other would be the defence lawyer. The Grubbling Brothers would plead guilty – not guilty – guilty but insane – slightly guilty. Then on Friday it was announced that the trial would start next Tuesday at the local assizes. Even in those days it was unusual for a trial to be arranged so soon after the crime. Apparently, however, it was considered a straightforward case; open-and-shut, in Sergeant Fagg's opinion.

Someone who had mixed feelings about all of this was Queenie Grubbling. Queenie was a loyal member of the Grubbling family. One of her tattoos read: 'Grubblings For Ever'. Nevertheless, with the brothers in jail, the sisters, Queenie especially, were having the time of their lives. On the day after the arrests, Queenie called a family conference and arranged for the printing of hundreds of leaflets:

The show goes on!
GRUBBLING SISTERS' CIRCUS
Still in business

On Friday there was a parade led by Queenie on the traction engine. This engine, rather like a colourful steamroller, was a big *at*traction in itself. That evening and on Saturday the circus was a sell-out.

ON SUNDAY, the Hickses went to church. The baby was heaved up the steps by willing members of the congregation. The choir, Horace and Phippy among them, took their places. The vicar advanced into his pulpit.

Alice soon found her attention wandering. She searched for unintended shapes in the stained glass windows. She waited for the peculiar vibrations in the pew when the deepest notes of the organ sounded. Beside her in the aisle, the giant baby gazed out from his pram. He yelled a couple of times during the first hymn and clapped his hands half-way through the sermon; otherwise he was as good as gold.

In many ways, from Alice's point of view, the most remarkable sight in church was Horace in his choirboy's surplice. His hair was slicked down, his mouth open in song and his expression — even with his black-patch glasses — guileless. But Horace wasn't singing. He had long since mastered the art of appearing to sing while doing something else. On this occasion what he was doing, below the level of the choir stalls, was organizing a swop: one cavalier on horseback for all or part of a younger choirboy's collection money. On Horace's left stood Phippy, while down in the congregation little Phippy tracked his brother's every move and longed to join him.

The sermon that day, as you might expect, concerned babies. 'My text,' said the vicar, 'is taken from Isaiah, chapter eleven, verse six: "And a little child shall lead them."'

Alice's thoughts drifted. She thought of Constable Dunkley coming round to collect his truncheon and telling her again what a brave girl she was. She thought of the welfare visitor, whose welfare visiting had been postponed (at the request of the police) until after the trial. She thought of the trial itself, two days away. She imagined the scene: the crowds and cameramen, the judge and jury, *the prisoners in the dock*. Then Basil Grubbling's gleaming confident smile rose up before her eyes and Alice felt a clutch of fear. She reached out for her mother's hand.

10

The Trial

IT WAS TUESDAY MORNING just before ten. Alice
sat with her father in the front row of the court facing
the judge's bench. On her right was the jury; on her
left, the witness-box, a press bench for reporters and the
dock with a row of little spikes around it.

The courtroom was packed. Horace and Ethel were
there with Auntie Joan, Phippy with his mum and dad,
the postman, Grandad Turner, the local reporter's
girlfriend (now fiancée) and many more. There was a
gallery, also packed, mostly with female members of the
Grubbling family, plus a considerable number of young
(presumably Grubbling) children.

Alice was excited and nervous. She glanced over her
shoulder and waved to Ethel. She stared up into the
vaulted ceiling of the courtroom. She squeezed a balled-
up hankie in her hand.

At ten o'clock the usher called for silence, the judge
took his seat and the trial began.

'Put up Basil Grubbling!' cried the clerk of the court.

Basil, smiling warmly, appeared in the dock.

'Is your name Basil Grubbling?'

'Yes,' said Basil.

'Basil Grubbling, you are charged that on the sixth of
May at four-thirty a.m. you did, without the consent of
his guardians, remove one large infant from number 42

Tucker Street. You are further charged with breaking and entering at the aforementioned address and the theft of a pram. How do you plead?'

'Not guilty,' said Basil, calmly.

Alice scowled. The fibber!

'Put up Hubert Grubbling!' cried the clerk.

One by one the Grubbling Brothers gathered in the dock (a box was provided for Lionel to stand on). Each pleaded not guilty, including Gus, who – technically – was telling the truth.

The prosecutor, Sir Walter Potter, rose to his feet. He adjusted a rather small wig on his rather large head. 'May it please your honour, ladies and gentlemen of the jury, I appear in this case for the prosecution, and my learned friend, er . . .' Sir Walter stared pointedly at the chairs intended for the defence counsel, which were unoccupied.

There was a commotion in the dock. Basil disappeared, then reappeared in the well of the court clutching a briefcase and a bundle of documents.

'It would seem, Sir Walter, that the defendants propose to represent themselves,' said the judge. 'Is that so?'

'It is, your honour,' said Basil. 'With your honour's permission.'

'And without it, I dare say.' The judge nodded to Sir Walter. 'Please continue.'

Sir Walter Potter outlined his case. It was, he declared, a terrible case, concerning as it did a gang of desperate men and one helpless, albeit somewhat large infant. Sir Walter gestured to an usher standing at the side of the court. A door opened and in came Mrs Hicks pushing a pram.

'This is that infant,' said Sir Walter.

There were gasps in the court and cries of pleasure, too.

'Ooh!'

'Ah!'

Alice leapt up and ran to her mother.

'My word, he *is* a whopper!' cried the judge.

Mrs Hicks took a seat next to Alice, with the attentive amiable baby parked in the aisle.

Sir Walter called his first witness: Sergeant Fagg. Sergeant Fagg, consulting his notebook, described the scene of the crime. He explained the probable method of entry and gave details of police inquiries. When the sergeant's evidence was completed, Basil rose to cross-examine.

'One moment,' said the judge. 'What's that on your head?'

'A wig, your honour.'

'You're not entitled to a wig. Take it off.'

Basil looked disappointed. 'I merely thought it would help the jury, your honour.'

'Well, it wouldn't. Please continue.'

Basil approached the witness-box. 'Good morning, Sergeant!'

'Er . . . good morning.'

'May I ask, did you by any chance attend the circus last week?'

Sergeant Fagg seemed puzzled. 'Yes.'

'Did you enjoy it?'

'. . . Yes.'

'Did you *pay*?'

'Objection!' Sir Walter leapt to his feet. 'This is irrelevant, your honour.'

'Sustained,' said the judge. 'Stick to the point, Mr Grubbling.'

Basil apologized. He thanked the sergeant, said, 'No further questions,' and resumed his seat.

The next witness was Constable Dunkley. Constable Dunkley was a young man and this was his first trial. In consequence, the buttons on his tunic gleamed and his face was flushed.

'Tell us, Constable, if you please, the circumstances of the arrests.'

'Sir.' Constable Dunkley cleared his throat. 'On Wednesday the sixth of May at eight-fifty p.m., acting on information received –'

And Alice thought, 'That's me!'

'– I, in the company of a fellow officer, entered the Big Top of the Grubbling Brothers' Circus.'

At this point there was a protest from the gallery.

'Objection!'

'And sisters!'

'Hear, hear!'

It was, of course, the Grubbling women and young girls, Queenie prominent among them.

The judge called for silence; Constable Dunkley continued. 'I discovered the defendants in the centre of the sawdust ring. I informed them of their rights and the reason for my presence. I told them they must come along with me.'

'What happened then?'

'The smallest of the brothers jumped on a box and

knocked my helmet off.'

'No, I never!' shouted Lionel.

'Silence!' cried the judge.

'A second brother attempted to run my colleague over in a pedal car, and a third squirted us with a hose.'

(Laughter in court.)

'I see.' Sir Walter waited for the laughter to subside. 'Thank you, Constable.' He turned to Basil. 'Your witness.'

Basil took a pair of spectacles from his pocket and perched them on his nose. There was nothing wrong with his eyesight, though; he thought it would impress the jury. 'Constable Dunkley, is it not the case that in this matter of the so-called arrest –'

'Objection, your honour. It was an arrest.'

'Sustained.'

'In this matter of the arrest, a perfectly *innocent* mistake occurred?'

'I don't know what you mean.'

'Didn't my brothers and I, in the heat and excitement of our performance, fall into the wholly understandable error of supposing that you and your unfortunate colleague were *part of the act*?'

'I . . .'

'Didn't the audience make the same error and applaud and cheer?'

'It was a very small audience.'

'Irrelevant!' Basil was in full cry now and getting the hang of things. 'Finally, didn't you yourself climb onto the very box you complained of earlier and take a bow?'

85

'Two bows!' shouted Lionel.

'Objection!' cried Sir Walter.

'Sustained,' conceded Basil. Then, 'I beg your pardon, your honour.'

'Don't mind me,' said the judge. 'Do you have any further questions for this witness?'

'Yes, your honour.' Basil removed a red ribbon from one of his documents (actually, an old laundry list). 'Constable, you have spoken of your visit to the circus. Will you tell the court: where was the giant baby at this time?'

'42 Tucker Street.'

'The home of Mr and Mrs Hicks?'

'Yes.'

'And *Alice* Hicks?'

'Yes.'

'Where was the pram?'

'The same place.'

'I see.' Basil studied his document. 'As regards the pram, did you find –' he turned to face the dock, '– Mr Hubert Grubbling's fingerprints on it?'

'No.'

'Mr Oswald Grubbling's?'

'No.'

'Mine?'

'. . . No.'

'Now then – think carefully before you reply. Did you find *Alice Hicks's* fingerprints on the pram?'

'Yes, but –'

'Thank you, Constable.' Basil smiled ingratiatingly at the jury. 'No further questions.'

86

There was a buzz in the court: a flurry of whispered remarks, a rustle of dresses. Mr Hicks took out his pipe, only to put it away when stared at by an usher. Horace left his seat and wriggled in next to Phippy. The giant baby lolled dozily in his pram. Alice swopped her balled-up hankie from one hand to the other.

Sir Walter, having conferred with his assistant and taken a sip of water, rose to his feet. 'Call Alice Hicks!'

'Alice Hicks!' called the usher.

Alice's heart pounded as she climbed the steps into the witness-box. The judge greeted her in a fatherly fashion and advised her to speak up. The clerk instructed her to take the book (the Bible) in her right hand and read from the card: I swear by Almighty God, and so on. Sir Walter came reassuringly towards her and asked a series of questions. In this way, Alice was able to provide a full account of the kidnapping and subsequent rescue of the giant baby. Her reasons for hiding out in the allotments, however, were only lightly touched on.

It was time for the cross-examination. Basil began benignly without even leaving his chair. 'Splendid! Well done!' He turned to Mr and Mrs Hicks. 'You have a clever daughter here.'

Mrs Hicks, despite herself, looked pleased.

Basil approached the witness-box. 'You told your story perfectly.'

Alice scowled.

'But it was a story – made up – wasn't it?'

'No!'

'We shall see.' Basil took a sip of water, having acquired this technique from Sir Walter. He pointed to the pram. 'Do you like this baby?'

'Yes, of course,' said Alice.

'Do you love him?'

'Yes!'

'Would you do *anything* for him?'

'Yes!'

'Would you tell lies for him?'

'Objection!' But Sir Walter was too late.

' . . . Yes,' said Alice (truthfully).

Basil adjusted his spectacles and glanced significantly at the jury. He proceeded to ask a number of questions about the allotments: how and when Alice had taken the baby there, who had assisted her and what her motives had been.

'So,' said Basil, gravely, 'to save the baby from the orphanage, you took him to the allotments.'

'Yes,' said Alice in a whisper.

'Speak up!'

'Yes!'

'Hmm.' Once more Basil adjusted his spectacles; it was becoming a genuine habit. 'Did you tell lies to your mother about it?'

Alice looked miserable. 'Yes.'

'Did you tell lies to your father?'

'Yes.'

'Constable Dunkley – Sergeant Fagg?'

'Yes.'

Basil shook his head, more in sorrow, it seemed, than anger. 'The thing is, Alice, where does lying stop and truth begin?' He waved a hand towards the dock. 'The fate of innocent men hangs on this distinction.'

That was the end of Basil's cross-examination. Alice, pink-faced and confused, joined her indignant parents at the front of the court. Basil resumed his seat and began sharpening a pencil. A pale and somewhat worried-looking Sir Walter remained deep in conversation with his assistant. Moments later, the court was adjourned for lunch.

11

The Verdict

OUT IN THE Town Hall gardens, Alice and her parents ate their sandwiches. Horace and Ethel had joined them (Auntie Joan had gone home), and Phippy and his family were nearby. The giant baby was lying back in his pram with his socks off playing with his toes. The hot blue sky was flecked with fluffy clouds. Fountains splashed in the centre of the gardens; sparrows and pigeons jostled for crumbs.

Alice was still seething. What a cheek that Basil had! He was the real fibber. She accepted a crisp from Ethel.

Ethel said, 'They're trying to make out you did it, y'know.'

'I know.'

'Like – straight from your house to the shed.'

'Yes.'

A sock flew out of the pram.

'Then put the blame on them.'

Horace and Phippy were playing marbles on the path.

'She should put the blame on them!' Phippy yelled. 'They did it.'

Horace took the opportunity to move his marble a little while Phippy wasn't looking. 'I wish I could be a witness,' he said.

Down in the cells, the Grubbling Brothers were

tucking in to a hamper of boiled mutton, veal pie, bread and cheese, pickled onions and scotch eggs, washed down with shandy. Also present were Mrs Grubbling and Queenie; Isobel was guarding the toddlers.

Considering the circumstances, the family were in good spirits.

'Seems to be going nicely,' said Mrs Grubbling. 'That Sir Potter bloke's looking worried.'

'Basil's got 'em on the run!' cried Lionel.

Only Oswald considered the blacker side of things. 'What worries me is, what if they find us guilty, anyway, and we go to jail?'

'You're in jail now!' cried Queenie.

'I mean afterwards, for ever like. What would we do then?'

'It's easy.' Basil waved his fork in a confident fashion. 'We'd break out.'

AT TWO O'CLOCK the court reassembled. Alice's evidence had concluded the case for the prosecution. Now it was the defence's turn.

'Call Hubert Grubbling!' commanded Basil.

When Hubert had taken the oath, Basil asked his first question. 'Hubert Grubbling, do you tell lies?'

'No,' lied Hubert.

'How tall are you?'

'Six foot, eleven and a half inches.'

'Are you sure of that?'

'Absolutely.'

Basil produced a tape measure and with an usher's assistance (and the judge's tolerance) measured Hubert.

The usher read out the figures. 'Six foot, eleven and a half inches.'

'Well, there we are,' said Basil. 'No dishonesty there.'

Now Basil called his other brothers and plied them with questions designed to show how honest *they* were. He asked Lionel how short he was, Oswald how heavy he was, and Gus what was the capital city of Venezuela, which Gus had conveniently written on the palm of his hand. Sir Walter protested at this irrelevant line of questioning, but the judge allowed it on the grounds that perhaps it was leading *somewhere*.

The brothers gave their evidence wearing much of the circus gear in which they had been arrested: painted eyebrows, a ginger wig, a green bowler hat with an enormous feather, vividly striped trousers and so on. This helped greatly with the other evidence that Basil encouraged them to provide; evidence, that is, of the work they did and the hours of dedicated practice it required, no time for kidnapping nonsense here. Thus, Hubert ended his visit to the witness-box with a clever

display of plate-spinning. Lionel presented his performing pigeons, who did card tricks. Oswald attempted and more or less managed to raise two of the ushers from the floor.

Again Sir Walter objected – 'This is a court of law, your honour, not a circus!' – and again the judge denied him. The fact was, the brothers were giving the performances of their lives. (Hubert had never not dropped a plate before.) The crowded courtroom much appreciated the show, especially as it was free. More to the point, the jury appreciated it, too; so did the judge.

And after the brothers came the sisters. Queenie was introduced as an alibi witness. She gave her evidence with a small angelic-looking Grubbling toddler in her arms as a sign of her good faith. When Sir Walter in his cross-examination cast doubt on her recollections of time and place, Queenie almost froze his blood with her stare.

Isobel dealt with the horse blanket found in the pram, a vital piece of prosecution evidence, or so it seemed. 'Yes, that's it!' she cried. 'I wondered where it had gone.' She went on to imply that the blanket had been pilfered from the circus: 'By kids, probably. They're always sneakin' in.'

Mrs Grubbling was called as a character witness. She spoke with genuine feeling of the 'moral superiority' of her boys. She dabbed a hankie to her eyes and sobbed persuasively when cross-examined.

Alice heard some of this evidence with exasperation, but missed some of it, too. It was becoming hot in the court. Cardigans and coats had been removed, newspapers were being used as fans. Alice felt drowsy.

Suddenly . . .

'Call the giant baby!'

Immediately, Sir Walter leapt to his feet. 'This is preposterous, your honour! How can a baby give evidence?'

'Why don't you wait and see?' said Basil. And to the judge, 'This witness is vital to the defence's case, your honour.'

The judge hesitated. 'Very well – no tricks, mind. Let's see how it goes.'

The baby, wide awake at this time, was wheeled into the well of the court. A particular hush descended on the courtroom. The reporters' pens were poised.

Basil stepped forward. 'Call Hubert and Lionel Grubbling!'

'What's this?' cried Sir Walter.

Basil gestured grandly towards the pram. 'A demonstration. I simply want the jury to see how this baby responds to his supposedly cruel kidnappers.'

Meanwhile, Hubert had reached the pram and was entertaining the plainly delighted baby with the feather on his hat. Lionel had climbed onto a chair and was having similar success with his revolving bow tie.

'See how terrified he is,' said Basil.

At this point Lionel got too close to the baby and was hauled into the pram.

'And helpless, too!'

That was the end of the defence's case (and nearly the end of Lionel). Basil did try to call one final witness –

himself — but got no further than, 'Now, Basil,' 'Yes, Basil?' before the judge told him (and his witness) to sit down and shut up.

AT THREE FORTY-FIVE, following a short adjournment, Sir Walter Potter, refreshed with tea and scones, rose to deliver his closing speech. 'Ladies and gentlemen of the jury, this trial is a contest between the good and the not-so-good, the police and the Grubbling Brothers, Alice Hicks and . . . this gentleman here. The facts are simple: a stolen baby, a gang of villainous men and a brave girl. You should attend to these and ignore the rest. Slapstick and circus antics have no place in a court of law.' Sir Walter took a sip of water and studied his notes. He continued speaking — outlining the evidence and urging the correct interpretation of it — for a further fifteen minutes. Then, with a flourish, he exhorted the jury to 'do their duty' and sat down.

Basil, refreshed with shandy and a mutton sandwich, took his place. He began quietly, addressing the jury as though they were his friends. He invited them to consider the perplexing business of lies and truth. He contrasted, with regret, the shining honesty of his brothers with the thoroughgoing dishonesty of the prosecution's main witness. She had lied, on her own admission, to everybody, so why not to them?

'Not that we should altogether blame her,' continued Basil. 'She's not a *bad* girl —'

'She's a good girl!' cried her mother.

'Her motives, indeed, were pure: to save the giant baby from the orphanage. Why, I might have done the same myself.' Basil sipped his water and regarded the jury over the rim of the glass. 'Of course, the only trouble is, she put the blame on others, as children sometimes will, bless 'em.'

Basil concluded his speech by reminding the jury of the legal difficulties involved in stealing a baby that did not, apparently, belong to anybody. He urged them not to blight the careers and devastate the lives of five innocent men, not to mention their poor old mother, on the doubtful evidence of one admittedly well-intentioned child. He sat down.

There was a scatter of applause from the gallery and also from Gus in the dock. The judge tapped lightly with his hammer. He shuffled a pile of notes in front of him and began his summing up.

HALF AN HOUR LATER: 'There we are, that is the position. You must attend to the facts, evaluate the evidence, forget the card tricks and consider your verdict.'

And so at four fifty-three p.m. the jury in the case of The King versus The Grubbling Brothers left the court-room. The judge returned to his rooms and put his feet up; the brothers returned to their cell and put up theirs. In general, the brothers were in buoyant mood. Basil had made a splendid case – 'He almost persuaded me!' cried Oswald – and their hopes were high. Only Basil, for once in his life, was pessimistic. For him the trial *had* been a contest – a game: Basil versus The King! Only now was he beginning to see the reality behind his courtroom performance; iron bars and wooden bunks, locks and loss of liberty. Yes, it was a game all right, but what if they lost?

At five-forty the jury returned. The judge was in his seat. The Grubbling Brothers were assembled in the dock. Alice, baby, mum and dad were in their places. All was quiet; so quiet that you could hear the squeak of the usher's boots, the drone of a wayward insect overhead.

The clerk of the court addressed the jury. 'Ladies and gentlemen of the jury, have you reached a verdict upon which you are all agreed?'

The foreman rose and faced the judge. 'Yes, your honour, we have.'

Now there was *utter* silence.

'Do you find the defendants guilty or not guilty?'

The foreman dabbed a handkerchief to the back of his neck, glanced down at a scrap of paper and said: 'Not guilty!'

12

Spy in the Grass

IT WAS LATE EVENING and this is what certain people (and one genius of a pigeon) were thinking:

Alice: The baby is *still* safe and not in the orphanage.

Mrs Hicks: The orphanage – oh, dear.

Mr Hicks: I've a good mind to keep him!

Horace: A cabbage shaped like Queen Victoria!

The Judge: That fellow with the plates was good.

The Foreman of the Jury: I think we might've made a mistake there.

Lionel's Star Pigeon: The ace of spades . . .

The Grubbling Brothers (except Basil): Free! Free!

Basil: Now what?

THAT NIGHT there was a remarkable storm of hailstones. It rattled on the roof so hard that Alice leapt up in bed anticipating burglars again, or the arrival of *another* baby. The hailstones, though big, like golf balls, broke no records, however, only some cucumber frames.

The next morning Alice woke up feeling exasperated but cheerful. It galled her to think of those dreadful brothers getting away with it. On the other hand she still had the giant baby. Also, there was the prospect of Norah's return.

At breakfast Alice noted her father's behaviour. When the baby was unaccountably fretful and close to tears, he sang 'Row, row, row your boat' to him. He spread Marmite on fingers of toast and fed him, too.

'You like that baby,' said Alice.

'Well . . .'

'You *love* him!'

'I suppose we're getting used to him,' said her mum.

'I was used to him straight away!' Alice declared.

Later that day, after school, Alice sat in the garden with the baby. Each of them had a lemon curd tart. The baby was pointing at the neighbour's cat as it crouched in the hedge.

'Da!'

Alice encouraged the cat to join them, without success.

Presently – 'Yoo-hoo!' – Auntie Joan arrived accompanied by Horace and a bag of knitting. With Alice's help, she held the knitting against the baby. 'My word, I do believe he's grown.' She laughed, but nervously. 'At this rate I may never catch him up.'

Mrs Hicks came out to join them.

Alice, who had earlier been playing with the baby, resumed her game. 'Watch this, Mum!' She tossed a ball, which the baby caught.

'Not bad.' Mrs Hicks wiped her hands on her apron. 'He'll make a good goalkeeper in a few years. Mind you, he could just lie there, couldn't he?'

Now Horace, his thoughts previously fixed on lemon curd tarts, took an interest. 'Do it again!'

Alice tossed the ball and once more the baby caught it.

'The knitting's coming on,' said Auntie Joan.

'Again,' said Horace.

Alice did as she was asked, but this time watching Horace. He had that gleam in his visible eye.

Then Norah Stubbs arrived: brown from her holiday and pink-faced, too, from running. She and Alice, like their mothers before them, had been friends since they were toddlers.

Norah sank to her knees on the grass. 'So this is him.'

'I hope so,' said Mrs Hicks.

'We found him!' cried Alice.

'I know – we heard about it.'

'How's your mother?' inquired Mrs Hicks. 'Did you have a nice time?'

'Lovely! She's all right. She's coming round.'

Norah felt in her pocket and handed Alice a present wrapped in tissue paper: a crinoline lady made from seashells. Mrs Hicks and Auntie Joan crowded in to admire it. Horace, meanwhile, picked up the ball . . . and tossed it to the baby.

ELSEWHERE, Hubert Grubbling was tossing a ball to a seal, which the seal – rather elderly now – was not catching. Lionel was hurling knives into Oswald's caravan door. Oswald and Gus were puzzling over the parts of a dismantled unicycle. Basil was immobile in a deckchair, smoking.

The brothers were despondent. The trouble was they had won the trial, but pretty well lost everything else. They didn't have the baby, nor did they have their self-respect: outwitted by a ten-year-old! Furthermore, they could not bear to have their stolen property stolen from them: the giant baby had become an obsession.

Hubert took a seat beside Basil. Lionel hurled his final knife and did likewise. Oswald and Gus came over too. The four of them gazed expectantly at their lounging brother. Gradually puffs of smoke like Indian signals began to rise more hopefully (ominously) from Basil's cigar. Finally, he leant forward and placed a hand on Lionel's shoulder. 'Lionel, I've got a little job for you.'

'What d'you mean, "little"?' said Lionel.

Basil merely smiled. 'Just listen – you'll love it.'

THE NEXT DAY was a half-holiday for the school. Alice had her lunch at Norah's, then the two of them went round to her house to play with the baby. When they arrived, they found Auntie Joan sitting in the garden, knitting.

'Your mum's popped out to have her hair done. I'm the baby-sitter.'

'Oh!' Alice went inside and came out again. 'Where's the baby?'

'*He's* popped out.' Auntie Joan raised a cup of tea to her lips. 'Horace and his pals – they took him for a stroll.' She heaved herself out of her chair. 'Would you like some pop?'

But Alice was already half-way down the path. 'Which way did they go?'

'How about a biscuit then?' Auntie Joan smoothed her skirt. 'To the park, I think, Horace said. Are you off? . . . He's a softy.'

ALICE AND NORAH raced to the park, through the gates, past the lodge, round the pond and up to the football pitch, where Alice's intuition told her Horace would be. He was there all right; so were thirty other boys, a dozen girls, four prams, three toddlers and a couple of dogs, one of them Horace's. A football match was about to begin.

Alice rushed to the giant baby's pram only to find it empty. With Norah's assistance, she pushed her way into a scrum of boys. There was Horace, and Phippy and Kenny, arguing with members of the opposing team. And there was the baby, sitting on the ground (in goal, actually).

The argument concerned the giant baby's eligibility to play.

'He can't play!'

'Yes, he can – he's from Tucker Street.'

'But he's a big kid.'

'Big kids not allowed!'

'He's not a big kid – he's a baby.'

'Use your eyes!'

'Shut your cake-hole!'

'Let him play!'

At this point, the row between Horace and the opposition became a row between Alice and Horace. Alice was fierce. She demanded to know what Horace was up to. Horace looked aggrieved. He claimed he was up to nothing and reminded Alice of all the things he had done for her lately – and the baby.

Alice wavered. What Horace said was true; furthermore, she had no wish to side with the Buff Street lot.

'Come on,' urged Kenny. 'He'll have some fun; he'll love it!'

'Be a sport,' said Horace.

FIVE MINUTES LATER the game started. In their first attack, Horace's team scored. In the other team's first attack, one of their players, with the goal at his mercy, was mesmerized by the giant goalkeeper and shot wide. In the next, he shot straight at him, after which there was a delay while the baby refused to let go of the ball. It took a session of 'This little piggy went to market' before they could continue.

Alice sat on a bench keeping an eye on things. She was accompanied by Norah and Ethel; Monica was in the team. Nearby, little Rosalind in a cowgirl's outfit was playing with another little girl. Horace's dog, his lead tied to the bench, was fast asleep under it. He had been coming to games like this since he was a pup, and had seen it all. A light wind ruffled the rhododendron bushes and the long grass that fringed the far side of the pitch. A train, invisible except for its flying steam, went rumbling by.

When the game had been going for twenty minutes and the score was 9–0, a loud cry of 'Penalty!' arose from the opposition. After much argument and a great rigmarole of pacing out the penalty spot, everything was ready. A hush descended on players and spectators alike. Then, just as the kicker commenced his run, the giant baby burped hugely, fell forward onto his hands and knees and *crawled* off.

Instantly, the penalty and indeed the entire game were forgotten.

'Look – he's crawling!'

'Crawling?' (This was Horace.) 'We've been carrying him around all this time and he can crawl?'

'Perhaps he's only just learnt.'

'Well he's got the idea now.'

'Look at him go!'

At remarkable speed and clearly delighted with himself, the giant baby crawled his way across the pitch and in and out of the flower beds. He was pursued by both teams and most of the spectators, with Alice overtaking everybody in her desire to reach him.

'Stop him!' she cried.

Crash went one of the benches.

'He'll hurt himself!'

Crunch went somebody's satchel.

'He'll hurt *us*!'

As he reached the path, the giant baby paused and pointed. 'Da!'

'He's stopped.'

But, no . . .

'He's started again!'

'Where's he going now?'
'Back down the hill!'
'Head him off!'
'Corner him!'
Eventually, at the edge of the brook the baby paused again.
'Sit on him,' said Horace, gasping.
Alice seemed doubtful. 'Shall I?'
'Yes – slow him down.'

Reluctantly (and willingly) she climbed onto the giant baby's back. Whereupon away he went, with Alice holding tight, up the pitch towards the tennis courts. The mob of more or less delirious children pursued and accompanied him, the noise of them fading only slightly as they cleared the brow of the hill. And the thought in Horace's mind was: 'Penny a ride!'

BACK at the bench, Horace's dog was awake and looking around. A pair of peacock butterflies spiralled by on the breeze. A dragonfly hovered. The scent of willowherb and marigolds was in the air, with a hint of soot from the trains. Down in the long grass a small head was raised. It was Lionel Grubbling, unconvincingly disguised (school cap, short trousers, close shave) as a boy. He took a notebook from his pocket, a pencil from the spine of the notebook and began to write.

13

Lost Letters

THE GIANT BABY'S fame was spreading. There were features on him in newspapers and magazines, and on the radio. On Friday evening Alice and Norah went to the cinema, and the newsreel had a whole item about him. He was shown in the garden with a pleased and embarrassed Mr and Mrs Hicks. (Alice had been at school at the time.) The audience cheered for the baby and booed for the Grubbling Brothers. One 'little boy', however, unnoticed on the back row, appeared to be doing the opposite.

Before the trial, scores of letters and cards had been delivered daily to the Hickses' house. After it, the red-faced, staggering postman began to arrive with them by the sackful.

On Saturday morning Mrs Hicks sat with a pile, endeavouring to deal with the backlog. Mr Hicks was dozing on the sofa. The baby was dozing, too, in his recently acquired playpen. Alice was playing with a Yo-Yo.

Mrs Hicks opened a letter. 'There's one here from another baby.'

'Really?' said Alice.

'Sort of . . . his mother wrote it. She wonders if he'd like a pen pal.'

'He'd like a playpen pal.'

Mrs Hicks put the letter aside and reached for another. 'This looks important.' Suddenly, her face turned pale and her hands shook.

'What's the matter?'

'It's this letter – they're coming to get him.'

'Who are?'

'The council!' Mrs Hicks read the letter aloud. '"A representative will call and remove the said infant –"'

'They can't!' cried Alice.

'"– remove the said infant on . . . Saturday, the six-teenth of May –"'

'That's today!'

'"Saturday . . . at ten-thirty a.m."'

Alice swivelled to the clock. 'That's now!'

Whereupon, strange but true, the doorbell rang.

Mr Hicks stirred.

Alice scuttled to the window. 'It's a woman – with a flowery hat on.'

'The representative, I'll bet.' Mrs Hicks was rousing her husband – showing him the letter – explaining the doorbell.

It rang again.

'Don't let her in!'

'Oh, Alice, we can't. Anyway, she'll come back.'

Alice stared wildly about. 'Let's hide him then!'

Surprisingly – perhaps they were panicked into it – Mr and Mrs Hicks went along with Alice's proposal. Mr Hicks procrastinated at the door – 'I'm coming! Just a minute!' – while Alice and her mum released the now wakeful baby and tried to hide him.

It was hopeless. The baby crawled under the table and

out again, behind the sofa and back, up the stairs and down. Meanwhile, Mr Hicks was doing valiant work:

'Sorry to keep you!'

'Won't be long!'

'Just putting my trousers on!'

The woman herself could also be heard.

'Open this door, please!'

'Be sensible, Mr Hicks!'

Finally, attracted by the offer of a doughnut, the giant baby was lured into the kitchen and from there into the pantry. Alice tossed his rattle and his rag doll in after him and shut the door.

'That's the best we can do.' Mrs Hicks smoothed her hair. 'Right, George – let her in.'

The woman from the council entered the house. She complained at being kept waiting, explained her business and asked to see the baby.

'So where is he?'

Mr Hicks looked puzzled. 'Who?'

'The baby, Mr Hicks.'

'Oh, him. I'm not sure. Have you see him, Marion?'

'Not lately.'

The woman, whose name was Mrs Butters, smiled ruefully. 'So . . . you're hiding him.' She glanced around. 'Where is he?' (raising the edge of the tablecloth) 'Under here?'

'Do you mind? That's a private table,' complained Mrs Hicks.

Mrs Butters looked behind the sofa – 'A private sofa!' – up the stairs and in the bedrooms – 'A private wardrobe!' – 'A private bed!'

Presently, she returned. 'You realize this is illegal; obstructing an officer of the council in her official duties? I shall have to file a report.'

Just then from the kitchen there came a loud, if muffled burp. Luckily, Mr Hicks had the presence of mind to pass it off – 'Pardon me!' – as his own. Unluckily, Alice and her mum had the same idea.

Mrs Butters glanced intently at each member of the family, and entered the kitchen. (Alice and her mum raised hands to their mouths in an identical nervous gesture.) There was a further sound from the pantry. Mrs Butters opened the door.

'And who is this?'

'Uncle Henry,' said Mr Hicks.

'Are you sure?'

'. . . No.'

'It's the baby,' said Alice, simply.

'My word, yes: the baby.' Mrs Butters shook her head. 'The baby and a half.' She crouched beside him. 'He's got a nice smile.'

'He's got a lovely left hook as well,' said Mr Hicks. 'Watch out for his rattle.'

Mrs Hicks gestured to her husband to be quiet. The baby crawled forward, clutching a Swiss roll he had acquired, and sat on the floor.

Mrs Butters continued to regard him. 'He reminds me of my Gerald, when he was little.'

Whereupon, Alice burst out, 'Please don't take him! He shouldn't go to an orphanage – he's got us!'

Mrs Butters rose to her feet. 'I'm sorry, dear, it's my job. I have to do it.'

'No, you don't!' cried Mrs Hicks.

'You tell her, Marion.'

'You don't *have* to do it.' Mrs Hicks was incensed. 'If this job of yours means taking defenceless babies from comfortable homes and putting them into orphanages, then all I can say is . . . don't!'

'But . . .'

'Think of little Gerald,' added Mr Hicks.

'Yes,' said Alice. 'How would he have liked it?'

'Oh dear!' Mrs Butters searched her bag for a hankie, but was handed one by Mrs Hicks. 'Thank you . . . (sob).' She wiped her eyes, considered her situation for a moment, and there and then resolved . . . *not* to do her job. 'I'll say I couldn't find him.'

'It's nearly the truth!' cried Alice.

After that Mrs Butters powdered her nose, shook hands with Mr and Mrs Hicks and departed.

HARDLY had Mrs Butters' car left Tucker Street than an enormous white removal van-cum-ambulance replaced it. And barely had Alice and her parents had time to celebrate their success, than the doorbell rang again.

Alice opened the door, delight still in her face. On the step stood a tall man in a white coat. He had cold blue eyes and thin lips. His hair was blond, almost white, so that his eyebrows and eyelashes were scarcely visible. He wore a pair of rimless spectacles and had what appeared to be a row of scalpels in his top pocket. He was carrying a clipboard.

'Doctor Splitter,' said the man.

Alice's smile disappeared. She stepped back into the house; the man followed. Encountering Mrs Hicks in the hall, he explained the reason for his visit.

'Mrs Hicks? Mrs Marion Hicks?'

'Yes.'

'Doctor Splitter. As I understand it, you have discovered a giant baby on your doorstep.'

'Well . . . yes.'

'In which case, scientifically speaking, he is not yours. I propose, therefore, to remove him to my laboratory.' Doctor Splitter consulted his clipboard. 'For certain . . . tests.'

'No!' cried Alice and her mum.

'Certain measurements . . . experiments . . . samples. Hmm. If you would sign this form.'

'No!'

'No?' Doctor Splitter seemed surprised.

'Yes, "no"!' said Mrs Hicks, angrily. 'That's the word.'

'It means, "we refuse",' added Mr Hicks, 'or – scientifically speaking – "buzz off"!'

Doctor Splitter remained unflustered. 'Did you not get my letter?'

'No!'

'What letter?'

'Never mind, I was prepared for that.' He removed an envelope from his pocket. 'Here is a copy.'

The letter was a disaster. It authorized R.T. Splitter, MD, FRS, PhD, PhD, PhD, to take possession of one large infant of the male sex currently residing at 42 Tucker Street. The wording was unambiguous and brutal. It allowed for no delays. It stressed the futility and illegality of any resistance on the part of the infant's present, temporary and entirely unofficial guardians. Worst of all, it was signed on behalf of His Majesty's Government by the Home Secretary. (Doctor Splitter, by the way – you might as well hear it now – was an extremely clever scientist, fairly famous and more or less mad. He did experimental work for governments, large companies and mad individuals like himself. His clients did not always know or care what methods he employed. It was results that counted.)

Alice and her parents read the letter, gasped, cried and stood firm.

'Well you can't have him!'

'You tell him, George!'

'Yes – push off!' yelled Alice.

But still Doctor Splitter remained calm. 'I was prepared for *that*.' He called out through the open door. 'Sergeant! Constable! It is as I feared. Please do your duty.'

Into the house stepped an embarrassed Sergeant Fagg and an apologetic Constable Dunkley. With obvious reluctance, they restrained the Hicks family while Doctor Splitter and his assistants transported the baby down the path and into the enormous van. The pram (plus baby) was raised into the back of the van by an electrical hoist and secured to the floor with leather straps.

Alice struggled in Sergeant Fagg's implacable grasp. She saw the baby's bewildered face as he rose up into the van. She saw his lip begin to tremble and the poignant way he clutched his rattle for comfort. She saw the

frightening collection of ropes, tools and scientific equipment that the van contained. She saw its doors begin to close.

Alice couldn't bear it. She kicked, struggled and, eventually, bit! The sergeant howled; Alice broke free and rushed down the path. The doors of the van were shut. Doctor Splitter was climbing into the passenger seat.

'Oh, no!' Alice was in floods of tears. 'Please don't take him – please!'

But Doctor Splitter was unmoved (he was no Mrs Butters). Confronted by Alice's appeal and her tear-stained, desperate face, the thought in *his* mind was: $Gb^3 = M^{0.386} + \pi\sqrt{\frac{m}{g}}$. He was, indeed, a soulless man.

Just then Horace arrived. He was in time to see the van move off, chased half-way down the street by Alice.

Meanwhile, from the opposite direction came Kenny. He was in time to watch the van go rumbling off up Stoke Street . . . and to take its number.

14

The Search

D OCTOR SPLITTER'S *van was in Dover Avenue passing the park gates.*

Alice raged back into the house. Sergeant Fagg was having his hand attended to by Mrs Hicks. Mr Hicks was on the phone. Alice heard nothing, saw nothing and raged out again. At the front gate she encountered Horace and Kenny.

'Hi, Alice!'

'What's up?'

'Everything!' In angry bursts she told them what had happened, wiping her tears on the sleeve of her dress as she did so.

Horace and Kenny were dumbfounded. Alice was called back in and told to apologize to Sergeant Fagg, who then with Constable Dunkley departed. Mrs Hicks stared forlornly at the playpen. She picked up a sheet of paper from the table – 'We never signed this form!' – and let it fall.

Mr Hicks was looking in the phone book. He had already phoned the Town Hall, without much luck. Now he was hoping to speak to his Member of Parliament. 'What a game. When we didn't want him, they wouldn't have him; when we do, they take him away.'

Doctor Splitter's van was climbing Harold's Hill on the outskirts of town.

Restlessly, Alice returned to the garden.

'Kenny got that van's number, y'know,' Horace said. (Kenny was a collector of car numbers.)

'What use is that?'

Horace wasn't sure. 'If we see it again, we'll . . . know it's the one.'

'I'll know, anyway.' Alice kicked furiously at the gravel path.

'Cheer up; all we need is a clue.'

'Yeah!' cried Kenny.

'Then we'll rescue him!' Horace was beginning to enthuse. 'We did it before, we can do it again. Have a look in the house.'

Back in the house, Alice drifted around. She went to the baby's room, then stood irresolutely in the kitchen doorway. She picked up the form from the table.

Alice started to read the form but was soon struggling. It was full of 'henceforths', 'forthwiths' and 'heretofores'. It appeared to be written in one continous sentence. One part, however, she could decipher. On a dotted line at the top were her parents' names and address. More importantly, a few lines below was *Doctor Splitter's name and address.*

THE ADDRESS WAS, 'The Abbot's House, Old Ford Road, Tippington'.

'I know Tippington,' said Kenny, softly. 'We had a scout camp there.'

'I remember!' Horace's good eye gleamed. And he said, 'Bikes!'

After a few more whispered words, the boys left. Alice went in to tell fibs to her mum. Mrs Hicks was folding nappies in the kitchen and looking miserable. Alice explained that she was going to Norah's now, as previously arranged (this bit was true). She couldn't bear to be in the house, she said, and would probably stay for tea.

'Try not to worry, Alice.' Mrs Hicks gave her a cuddle. 'We'll do what we can.'

Alice departed, taking her bike from the side of the house and pushing it down the path. Her dad appeared in the doorway and waved.

Doctor Splitter's van was bumping along a narrow country lane.

Alice told Norah what had happened, Norah told *her* mum a few fibs and the girls rode off to meet Horace and Kenny. Ethel was missing. She had gone with Monica and her mum to get Monica a pair of shoes. Phippy wasn't there either. He had caught the mumps two days earlier and was presently shut up in his room, with little Phippy (naturally).

When the girls reached the park gates, the boys were waiting. Kenny, who had no bike of his own, had borrowed his brother's.

Horace gestured to his saddlebag, which was bulging. 'Got a few things.'

'Me, too,' said Kenny.

'How far is it?' asked Norah.

Kenny frowned. 'It's up Harold's Hill and then . . .
I'm not sure.'

'We were in a bus last time,' added Horace.

Soon they were off, up Dover Avenue, up Pear Street
towards the outskirts of the town. It was half-past two.
The sun was shining, but with a curious green tinge; the
sky, though mainly blue, was mauve and almost purple
in places. Newspapers had reported sun spots and solar
flares in the past few days. Peculiar weather was fore-
cast. (Coincidentally, 'Strange But True' that week had
contained an account of an amazing shower of *live fish*
which had fallen on Omaha, Nebraska earlier in the
year.)

When the cyclists reached Harold's Hill, they dismounted and walked. At the top they rested on the grass
verge. Traffic was lighter in those days; fewer cars, more
bikes.

Horace produced a bottle of ice-cream soda, took a
swig and handed it on.

Norah said, 'How much further? Where are we?'

Kenny gazed into the distance. 'It's over that way . . .
I think.'

'We should be going,' Alice said.

*Doctor Splitter's van was pulling up in front of a huge
Elizabethan mansion.*

In the increasingly purple sky, a couple of gulls soared
and swooped. Up ahead, Alice and the others could see
open countryside, little clusters of houses, electricity
pylons, trees and telegraph poles. Behind them lay the
town. Smoke was rising from the brickworks' chimneys,

and steam from a train in Buff Street Station. On the edge of the town in Cummings Fields, a tiny Big Top was clearly visible with a cluster of toy caravans around it.

'There's the circus!' Horace cried, beginning to pedal away. 'Wonder what *they're* up to?'

THE GRUBBLING BROTHERS were up to quite a lot. Earlier, Lionel (school cap, stubbly chin) had witnessed the removal of the giant baby. (*He* had taken the van's number, too.) Gus had been dispatched to tell Basil. Basil had exploded: who was this pinching *their* baby from those that had pinched him back from them in the first place? Then Basil had leapt onto his motorbike, with Hubert folded up in the sidecar, and away they'd sped to see for themselves. Lionel was still telling them the story, when Alice was observed to ride away. Thereafter, effectively disguised in helmets and goggles, Basil and Hubert had stuck to the trail.

Beyond Harold's Hill the road swung away into an avenue of trees. There was a stone bridge, so covered in moss it hardly could be seen. Past the bridge, Alice noticed a signpost saying: Tippington 2 miles. Past the signpost, Kenny got a puncture.

Doctor Splitter was sitting down to a plate of poached eggs on toast.

Fixing the puncture took twenty minutes. Alice had a puncture outfit in her saddlebag. Horace borrowed a bowl of water from a nearby cottage to detect the leak. Norah supplied the only functioning pump. Alice, impatient to be off, rode on a little way and found another signpost: Tippington 1 mile. Eventually, they followed this. But then the road divided with no sign this time to show which branch led where. Presently, it divided again. All the while the roads themselves were narrowing. It was as if the first big road was fraying, like a piece of rope. After a time, Alice dismounted, hurling her bike onto a grassy bank. The others followed suit. They were caught in a maze of narrow lanes and high hedges, and absolutely as lost as they could be. (Actually, Basil and Hubert were lost as well, not to mention being stuck behind a flock of sheep.)

'This is hopeless.'

'No, it's not!'

'Where *are* we?'

'We should've took that other turning.'

'Let's ask somebody!'

'Who, though?'

Doctor Splitter was cleaning his teeth.

Around a bend in the lane, a small white van appeared. It was travelling slowly, making a terrible racket.

'A van!' cried Horace.

Instantly, the four of them slid below the bank and peered up over it. The van crawled noisily by.

'It's like a baby of the big 'un,' said Kenny.

'Could you recognize him?' Horace was referring to the driver.

Alice shook her head. 'I'm not sure.'

'He had a white coat on . . . I think,' said Norah.

They turned to watch the van go down the lane. Whereupon, though its noise was audible still, it disappeared. The children scrambled up and ran. Reaching the spot where the van had vanished, they found a driveway all overhung with brambles and wild roses. The van would have needed to *push* its way in.

At the side of the drive were two signs: one, ancient and weathered, saying, The Abbot's House ('Found it!' cried Horace), the other recently painted (red on white), saying,

Trespassers will be Prosecuted
NO UNAUTHORIZED PERSONS
KEEP OUT!

Alice, with the others close behind, went in.

The giant baby was being strapped into a curious chair in Doctor Splitter's laboratory.

A few yards down the drive, the children found an enormous pair of gates set in a stone wall. They scaled the wall using their bikes to stand on, struggled through an undergrowth of ferns and nettles and entered a thicket of elderberry bushes. Clouds of tiny flies rose up to meet them. A flurry of wood pigeons made them jump. The sky above was barely visible. They were lost again.

Alice sat on the ground shaking flies from her hair. Horace was scratching his numerous nettle stings. Norah and Kenny were independently preparing to admit defeat. Then, close by, a car door slammed.

The children crept forward. Parting the branches of a myrtle bush, they saw ahead, across a gravel drive, a huge dilapidated house. Its walls were lichen-covered limestone, its windows of leaded glass. It had a ruined clock tower above its central porch, and towering chimneys. Glancing left and right, Alice and the others scuttled towards the nearest window.

Doctor Splitter's assistants were lowering a metal skull-cap down onto the giant baby's head.

They peeped in. It was a mighty kitchen with four sinks, tremendous racks of plates, a massive fireplace and hooks embedded in the ceiling. But it was empty. They crept to the next window, again an empty room; only a suit of armour, shields and spears on the walls, a chandelier. And the next was a library with shelves of books from floor to ceiling. And the next . . .

Doctor Splitter was adjusting a dial on his control panel.

. . . was a laboratory.

'Oh!' Joy and consternation combined in Alice's heart as her gaze fell on the baby. He was strapped into a kind of dentist's chair. Doctor Splitter's assistants were on either side of him. Doctor Splitter himself was seated at a row of glowing dials.

The children stared at the appalling scene and wondered what on earth to do. Run for help, perhaps, or . . .

Doctor Splitter's third *assistant stepped up behind a bunch of nosy kids and grabbed them.*

'Help!'

15

Doctor Splitter's Laboratory

OCTOR SPLITTER'S assistant was big, but not so big that he could hold onto four children who were determined to get away. No, he could only hold onto two: Horace and Norah. Alice and Kenny, however, made no effort to escape but joined in the struggle, leaping on the man's back and kicking his shins. If the other assistants hadn't arrived, who knows what might have happened. As it was, the children were overpowered and frog-marched into the house.

Here they now stood, struggling still, in Doctor Splitter's vast laboratory. It had an imposing barrel-vaulted ceiling. The ancient floor was covered in linoleum. There were five workbenches equipped with sinks, taps, gas taps and Bunsen burners. There were shelves of chemicals in glass jars and cupboards full of preserved specimens. There was an entire human skeleton dangling from a brass stand. There was a Wilson cloud chamber in one corner and a Van de Graff generator in another. There was something which looked as though it could have been there since the house was built, for it resembled a torturer's rack. There was an electric furnace and a circular saw.

Alice took in little of this; she only had eyes for the giant baby. He remained strapped in his chair with the skullcap suspended above his head. He was yelling and

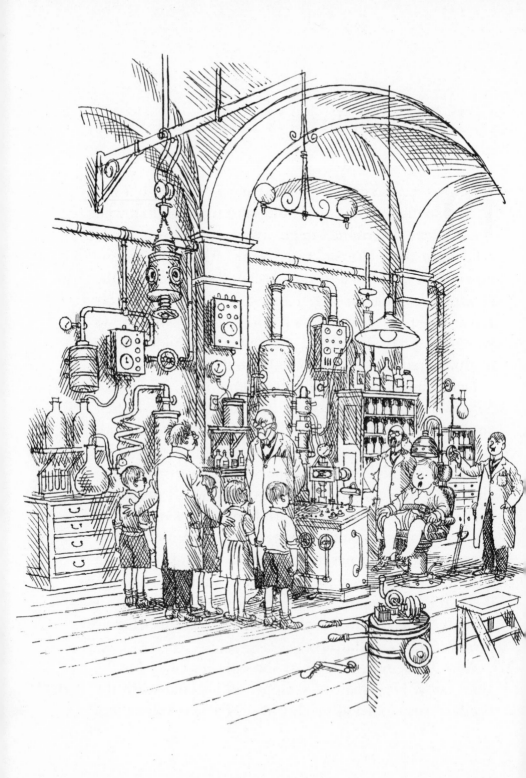

wriggling about, as far as he was able, for *he* had spotted Alice.

Doctor Splitter scrutinized his visitors. There was a look of clever madness in his eyes and a smell of formaldehyde about him, and toothpaste.

'Who have we here? Ah, yes – the daughter of the house.'

'We're gonna tell on you!' Norah blurted out.

'Yes!' cried Horace. 'Torturin' babies!'

Doctor Splitter was unmoved. 'Maurice – ropes.'

While the children were being tied up, each to a chair, Doctor Splitter strolled thoughtfully about. He raised the lid of a vibrating canister, opened and shut the door to the electric furnace and washed his hands at the nearest sink.

'Now – how did you get here?'

Silence.

'What means of locomotion?'

Silence still.

'Hmm. Then I shall work it out.' Doctor Splitter stared evenly at his prisoners as though intent on reading their thoughts. He looked at his watch. A thin smile appeared on his face and, 'Bicycles!' he declared.

The children's expression informed him he was right. Alfred and Charles, the other assistants, were dispatched to find the bicycles and hide them in the cellar.

'Otherwise,' said Doctor Splitter, 'someone – the police, for instance – might foolishly suppose their owners were nearby.'

'Bicycles go missing all the time, sir,' said Maurice.

'Children too,' said Doctor Splitter.

TOP SECRET

Doctor Splitter's assignment: Doctor Splitter's hush-hush assignment from the government was to extract, by whatever means proved necessary, a *growth formula* from the giant baby. (If you are surprised that a government could employ such a man for such a purpose, don't be.) The military significance of the baby was considered to be immense. A successful formula could lead to giant soldiers, sailors and airmen; giant legs of lamb, for that matter. The project's code name was: 'Goliath'.

WHEN Alfred and Charles returned, Doctor Splitter left. Maurice left also by another door. The children were mightily scared, their heads buzzing with such thoughts as, 'Oh, mother!' and, 'Look at that skeleton!'

Alfred began heating a beaker of colourless liquid.

Alice said, 'When did you feed him? He needs plenty to eat, y'know.'

'That's classified information,' said Alfred.

'When did you change his nappy?'

'That's classified, too. He's a top secret baby.' Alfred selected a jar from a shelf and removed its lid.

Horace addressed the other assistant, Charles, who was lifting a steel box down from a cupboard. 'What kind of doctor is he?'

'He's a clever 'un. Pays well.'

'Doctors are supposed to cure people,' said Norah, tearfully, 'not tie them up.'

Alfred was pouring the now bubbling liquid into a second beaker containing a measure of dried leaves. Charles was opening the box. Presently, the pair of them sat down to smaller beakers of steaming tea and a Petrie dish of arrowroot biscuits.

Alice said, 'The baby likes arrowroot biscuits,' but got no response.

After a time, Charles stood up, brushing the crumbs from his coat. 'Let's show 'em the tortoise!'

'You show 'em,' said Alfred.

Charles hesitated, glancing uneasily towards the door. He reached beneath a bench and produced a cage with a tortoise in it. (The tortoise had the number '4' painted on its shell.) Charles carried the cage to the far end of the laboratory and placed it on the floor.

'Watch this!'

Quick as a blink, out shot the tortoise. At preposterous speed, it hurtled back up the gangway between the benches and clattered into the base of the Wilson cloud chamber.

'There!' Charles's face was suffused with pride and glee. 'What d'you make of *that*?'

The tortoise was spinning like a top on the linoleum floor. It must have learnt to withdraw its head just before impact. Alice and the others, despite their plight, were fascinated.

'Did Doctor Splitter . . . ?' asked Kenny.

'Yes!' Charles was replacing the tortoise in its cage. 'Told you he was a clever 'un.' He turned to Alfred. 'Let's show 'em the hedgehog!'

BUT THE HEDGEHOG was not revealed (not then, not ever), for at that moment Doctor Splitter returned; Maurice also. Charles, flustered and fearful, made a hash of replacing the cage. 'Sir . . . I was, er . . . Alfred told me to do it.'

'No, I didn't!'

Doctor Splitter said nothing; he hardly needed to. He was the kind of man who put the fear of God (or the devil) into others with the merest twitch of his almost invisible eyebrows.

Doctor Splitter resumed his seat at the control panel. 'Maurice – lights.' The sky outside was continuing to darken. 'Let us proceed.'

'What about these kids, sir?'

'Let – us – proceed.'

Adjustments were made to various items of equipment wired up to the chair. Switches were thrown, dials manipulated, screws turned. The children watched with mounting horror. There was a hum of machinery seeming to come from the chair itself. A blue light lit up the baby's ever more anxious face.

'Lower the Y-ray oscillator,' said Doctor Splitter.

The skullcap began to descend.

Alice could not contain herself. 'Stop it!'

'Yes – leave him alone!' cried Norah.

The cap was down upon the baby's head.

'Adjust the piezo ignitor,' said Doctor Splitter.

Alfred did something to a copper disc.

'Plug in the Zartmann coil.'

Alice was going crazy. She kicked and struggled in her chair, almost toppled over. Meanwhile, unnoticed by anybody, a frightened face – Hubert's! – appeared at one of the windows, observed the scene and vanished. Then the weather took a hand. Outside, the sky was almost black and it was only half-past four. A lacework of green lightning – no thunder – was leaping about above the trees. With a surge, it simultaneously lit up the windows and fused the lights. When the emergency generator came on, it interfered with that as well, causing the lights to flicker.

With a plaintive cry, the giant baby lurched sideways, broke free of his straps and inadvertently knocked Maurice to the floor. Soon all three assistants were struggling to restrain him.

Alice saw her chance. 'Let me – you're only scaring him more!'

Doctor Splitter was decisive. 'A sensible proposal. Maurice – release her.'

Alice rushed headlong at the giant baby, where she received a welcoming smile and a sort of goldfish kiss, which she had lately taught him. Alice kissed him back and patted his dimpled hand. Alfred, Charles and Maurice stood uncertainly by.

Doctor Splitter said, 'Maurice – spare straps.'

Then Alice thought of something. Impulsively, she grasped the baby's shoulders and heaved. Hanging on and falling backwards, she succeeded in raising him up, out of the chair and down onto the floor. Fortunately, the baby landed on his hands and knees, and Alice was unflattened.

The assistants were stunned.

'What's this?'

'Stop her!'

'Never mind her – stop him!'

For, of course, all set and wound up so to speak in his crawling position, the giant baby was off, not as fast as the tortoise, perhaps, but harder to stop. Alfred, Charles and Maurice pursued him down the gangway. Doctor Splitter pursued them.

Alice had not planned this opportunity to release the others, but she took it all the same. After which, *they* joined the chase. Up one gangway and down the next the giant baby crawled. Lab stools were brushed aside and the human skeleton went flying. The tortoise escaped, too. The lights continued to flicker, lightning scribbled across the sky and a rising wind was beginning to rock the trees.

'Head him off!'

'Corner him!' the assistants cried. (It was the park all over again.)

But the gangways were narrow and the baby was wide; the light poor and the noise considerable, so that Doctor Splitter's calm instructions, for instance, were not heard. Yes, the confusion was total, and that was before Alice and the others took a hand. The first thing *they* did was to dodge round the other way – 'It's them kids!' – open a door – 'Grab 'em!' – usher the baby through – 'There they go!' – and slam the door behind them.

They were in a darkened library. The giant baby rampaged across the carpeted floor. In the gloom, he collided with and partially demolished a couple of eighteenth-century chairs.

'Where now?' the children cried.

'This way!'

'Come on!'

Horace and Norah pushed over a bookcase to cover their retreat. Right on their heels, Maurice neatly skidded to a halt, only to be bowled over by Alfred and trodden on by Charles.

The next room had spears and shields on the walls, which Kenny was all for grabbing. But the weapons were too high, the pursuers too close.

'Keep going!'

'They're gonna get us!'

'Oh, mother!'

Now they were in the enormous kitchen with its tremendous racks of plates and massive fireplace. Unluckily, the giant baby decided to have a breather. He sat on the floor and wouldn't budge. Then the far door opened and the flickering figure of Doctor Splitter was revealed; he had cunningly outflanked them. Doctor Splitter had a flashlamp in his hand and something dark and bulky over his other arm.

Seconds later, in rushed Alfred and Charles, with Maurice limping behind. The dismayed yet still defiant children gathered protectively around the baby. Horace gripped a plate and prepared to throw it. Charles said, 'Gotcha!'

There was a pause. In the silence, Alice could hear the wind in the trees. From the depths of the house, the emergency generator rumbled and throbbed. There was a cough from Kenny; a muffled sneeze from Charles.

Suddenly – CRASH! – an antique garden tub with a small orange tree in it (and a small orange on *it*) came hurtling through the window. Doctor Splitter shone his lamp in the direction of the gaping hole, Charles ducked down beneath the kitchen table and Norah screamed. Whereupon, in through the windy gap, like Robin Hood, leapt Basil Grubbling, with Hubert clambering after.

It was now a quarter to five and this is what some of the occupants of the kitchen, plus one other, were thinking:

Alice: Is this a good thing or a bad thing?

Horace: Whose side is he on?

Doctor Splitter: Hmm – more visitors.

Charles: Oh, mother!

Basil: I think I've pulled a muscle.

Hubert: Now what?

Phippy (in his bedroom): I'm bored.

Well, Basil and Hubert were there to save the baby, though who they were saving him *for* was not so certain. They joined the children, organized a swift retreat to the nearest plate rack and defied 'the barmy doctor and his mob' to do their worst. Doctor Splitter tried to negotiate – 'I am working for the government, you know' – but Hubert threw a plate at him, resisting, no doubt, the urge to juggle with it first. Then Horace threw one at Maurice, Norah one at Alfred, and Charles half a one at no one in particular.

The children were wary of their new-found allies. Alice, especially, could not decide who to keep an eye on. Desperate times, however, require desperate measures.

The battle of the plates, and cups and saucers, and soup tureens continued. Alfred and Charles fetched shields from the other room, but (sanely) left the spears where they were. Maurice tried creeping along under the table, only to be hit on the head as he emerged by the baby wielding a saucepan. But if the defence was holding up, retreat or escape with a crawling baby across a glass- and plate-strewn floor was out of the question.

Then Doctor Splitter took charge. He climbed onto the table – 'Enough of this!' – whirled a dark and spreading something or other above his head and cast it over his unruly opponents. It was ... a net ('Gotcha again!' cried Charles), cunningly devised by the doctor himself to combine maximum strength with maximum entanglement. The best thing to do when caught in a net, apparently, is *not* to struggle. Alice and the others struggled considerably before this thought occurred to them. Thereafter they collapsed in an exhausted heap.

Things were becoming *really* serious. Doctor Splitter sent Alfred off for his bag. Charles stood nearby with a rolling-pin. Maurice groaned from beneath the table. Alfred and the bag returned. Doctor Splitter took it, peered inside, felt around and withdrew a horribly large hypodermic syringe. 'Our visitors have become too energetic, Alfred.' He plunged the needle into a small glass jar.

'Yes . . . sir,' said Alfred.

'We must subdue them.' Doctor Splitter drew up into the syringe a quantity of amber liquid. He held it aloft against the available light and squirted a tiny fountain into the air. He approached his prisoners in the net.

At which point, the following events occurred:
Alice, Basil and the others kicked up a dreadful racket and struggled violently.

Charles, panicked by Doctor Splitter's mad intentions, ran off and hid in the cellar.

Doctor Splitter told Maurice to shine his lamp on the net.

There was a monumental thud at the front of the house, like quarry blasting.

The chandelier crashed to the floor in the next room.

Alfred ran off and hid in the cellar.

Queenie Grubbling – big, brave and unstoppable – came charging into the kitchen.

Maurice was knocked unconscious with his own lamp.

Alfred and Charles inadvertently terrified each other in the darkened cellar.

Doctor Splitter, still cool and calm, was captured.

THERE WAS GREAT RELIEF in the crowded kitchen. Lionel and Oswald appeared and began to untangle the net. Queenie kept a firm hold on Doctor Splitter. Maurice lay insensible on the floor. Everyone talked at once:

'Who's she?'

'It's Queenie Grubbling.'

'Good old Queenie!'

'I thought you'd never get here!'

'What was that big bang?'

'I'm famished!'

'Da!'

Queenie, it seemed, with passengers Lionel and Oswald, had arrived by traction engine (Basil having gone for help on his motorbike). She had rammed the main gates, demolished the porch and flattened the front door. Now she had Doctor Splitter in her powerful grip, prior to rolling him up in his own net as soon as it became available.

Once released, Alice rushed off and returned with the pram. The baby was dusted down and hoisted in. Alice watched, warily again, as Hubert offered him a carrot and Queenie tickled his chin. It occurred to her how oddly things had worked out. If the Grubbling Brothers had gone to jail, *as they deserved*, none of this would have happened.

In the meantime, Horace was expressing his joy by throwing a few more plates. Kenny and Norah had discovered the pantry and were raiding it. A scatter of moths, deceived by the darkness and drawn by the light, flitted about in the dusty air. The wind outside was dying down . . . and a tortoise was fleeing the house.

16

Consequences

YES, ONE THING does lead to another. The jury's verdict had led to Lionel's spying, which in turn had led to Basil's motorbike surveillance and Queenie's thunderous rescue. And that was only the beginning. The consequences continued to flow: for Alice and her parents, the giant baby, Horace, the Grubblings, Doctor Splitter and his assistants, and many more.

Consequences for Alice

For Alice the rescue meant relief, followed by a period of watchful unease until the police and the local reporter arrived. Only when the photographs were being taken did she begin to relax. Only when she arrived home did she feel really safe.

Further consequences for Alice included lots of attention at school and a huge amount of fun (and jelly) at the street party. Street parties were not uncommon in those days (less traffic). This one was organized by Alice and Norah's mums to celebrate the baby's return and the bravery of his rescuers.

The giant baby sat in the place of honour at the head of a row of tables set out in the street. Alice, her friends and cousins, a number of neighbours' children, the postman's two little girls and the local reporter's fiancée's younger brother occupied the remaining places. The food was supplied by the editor of the local paper. Sergeant Fagg and Constable Dunkley were in attendance in paper hats. They served the jelly and redirected the traffic.

During the party, the Grubbling Brothers arrived. They distributed 'big baby' balloons, which somebody had begun to produce, and staged an impromptu performance. Basil made a speech.

Phippy, by the way, although he missed the party, didn't miss the food. Towards the end, the performance became a parade. When the crowd passed noisily down Phippy's street, there was Phippy, still quarantined, leaning out of his window. Ashamed that they had forgotten him, Horace and Kenny ran back to gather a

basket of left-overs. Hubert, Lionel and Oswald re-enacted their human tower. They raised the basket up to Phippy's grateful grasp (and little Phippy's).

Consequences for the Giant Baby

The main consequence for the baby was that he became more famous than ever. His photograph was in all the newspapers, all over again; his story on everyone's lips. A considerable sum was offered by one paper for his autobiography. The fact that he couldn't write or talk seemed to be no hindrance. Mr and Mrs Hicks said they would think about it.

Other proposals included a 'giant baby' board game, a 25,000-piece 'giant baby' jigsaw puzzle and a 'giant

baby' novelty teapot. The idea of a musical play, in which, quite possibly, the baby himself would star, was also being considered.

Consequences for Doctor Splitter

Doctor Splitter was locked up. Six weeks later, there was a trial at which Alfred, Charles and Maurice turned king's evidence. He then got five years and they were placed on probation. Doctor Splitter, for his part, simultaneously denied everything and said that he was working for the government. The government had hopes of hushing things up. But photographs in the papers of Doctor Splitter's laboratory soon put paid to that. Subsequently, the *government* denied everything. Any documents from Doctor Splitter were forgeries, any statements from Doctor Splitter were lies and, anyway, who *was* Doctor Splitter?

One fortunate consequence of all this was that the Home Secretary felt obliged to write to Mr and Mrs Hicks. He praised their staunchness in adversity and hoped they would continue with their excellent care of the giant baby, 'for the foreseeable future'.

Consequences for the Grubblings

The Grubbling Brothers were changed men (except Gus). They had embarked on a course of action with definite criminal possibilities and ended up as heroes. But it had been touch and go. Even as he was hurling the plant tub through the window, Basil still had thoughts of rescuing the baby and running off with him. What changed his mind or, better still, his heart, it is hard to tell. Perhaps, as he leapt in through the window and despite his pulled muscle, Basil just felt like a hero. Kenny, who failed to recognize him, had cheered; maybe that did it.

Anyway, Basil inadvertently slipped into the hero's role and found he liked it. (The children at the party might not listen to his speech but they wanted his autograph.) The other brothers mostly followed Basil's lead. Hubert, though, to be fair, had harboured no bad thoughts when he had come to the rescue. Gus (there has been no opportunity to mention this before), missed the entire thing. He had been at the cinema on the afternoon in question. Actually, he missed most of the film, too, having accidentally locked himself in the lavatory.

Queenie, the heroine of the whole affair, was less affected. The big change in her life had come from running the circus when the brothers were in jail. All the same, Queenie received her share of attention and was glad of it. She lined the interior of her caravan with cuttings from the papers. When an invitation came to open the church bazaar, Queenie did it in style on the traction engine.

The other big change for the Grubbling family was financial. Because of the publicity, crowds had returned and offers were pouring in from all parts of the country. Oswald and Isobel mapped out a tour that would keep them occupied for months. Basil, now, smoked only the finest cigars and his smile was broader than ever. Oh, yes, to be doing well and (more or less) to *deserve* it – there was a happy ending indeed.

LATE ONE EVENING, a few days after the rescue, Alice, Norah and the giant baby sat together in the park. It had been a particularly scorching day. Tar had melted on the roads; pomegranates were ripening in the Town Hall gardens. The giant baby in his gentleman's sun hat was lolling on the grass, sucking his fist. Norah was fanning him with a dock leaf.

Nearby, two tribes of boys plus a few girls were playing football. It was a replay of the abandoned match. Horace had been much upset on that occasion, his side was winning 9–0. Now, however, the score was 34–12 and Horace was in heaven. The main difference between the teams was a solidly-built, boundlessly-energetic, *stubbly-chinned* centreforward: Lionel.

On the touchline, Ethel, Monica and little Rosalind were doing a leisurely version of some maternity exercises, which Ethel had found in *The Motherhood Book*. That book, by the way, was another example of consequences. All over the town now parents were being rebuked by older children for not cleaning their babies' teeth, the virtues of Beezley's Safety Prams were preached, and the benefits of flannel nightgowns. In many homes, too, dummies mysteriously disappeared. For in *The Motherhood Book* it plainly stated that, 'Although a popular invention, the "comforter" or "dummy" is wholly bad and quite unnecessary for a baby.'

Alice was sitting on a bench watching the baby. Norah had plucked a buttercup and was holding it beneath his chin. The baby rolled over and lurched up.

He grabbed the bench and hauled himself to his feet, a skill he had recently acquired. Despite Alice's efforts to stop him, he proceeded to chew the top rail. Suddenly, a curious, almost wistful expression appeared on his face. He threw his head back and gazed intently at the empty sky.

MORE EVIDENCE of the baby's chewing was to be found in the top rail of his playpen. That night, while Alice was having her bath and the baby his supper, Mr Hicks noticed the marks.

'What's all this?'

'It's him,' said Mrs Hicks. 'He's teething.'

'Teething?'

'Yes, I think so. Take a look.'

'You take a look.' Mr Hicks sat at the table. 'It'll be like a lawn-mower in there.'

'No, you'll be all right. Put your finger in.'

'Not likely!' Mr Hicks examined his hand. 'I'm fond of my fingers.'

A little later, Alice came down in her pyjamas. The giant baby was put to bed, holding his arms up high to help in his own undressing – another skill recently acquired. Mrs Hicks brushed Alice's hair.

Presently, a game of Snap was proposed by Alice and unsuccessfully resisted by her dad. Soon . . .

'Snap!' yelled Alice.

'That's cheating,' grumbled Mr Hicks.

'No it's not,' said Mrs Hicks. 'Snap!'

'Yes it is. You two say snap before you see the card.'

'No, we don't,' said Alice. 'We're just –'

'Snap!' yelled her mum.

'– quick.'

Mr Hicks continued to grumble. 'I dunno, seems fishy to me.' He gave a start and pointed to the window. 'What's *that*?'

Alice and her mum turned.

'Snap!' yelled Mr Hicks, triumphantly.

'Dad!'

'George!'

'Well . . .'

IT WAS LATE; past midnight. The upstairs windows of the house were open wide. A sultry breeze disturbed the curtains and the fragrance of night-scented stock filled the air. In the sky an unusual flickering light had begun to show. It stretched in a luminous band of green and white in a high arc above the town.

Alice sat bolt upright in bed. Something was wrong; she knew it. Perhaps it was the flicker of light that had disturbed her, or her intuition, or . . . the half-familiar sound she now could hear outside her door. Alice tiptoed to the door and opened it. On the landing, clutching the banister, stood the giant baby, his gaze fixed on the skylight, which was also open. He appeared to be . . . listening.

Alice listened too. What could she hear? The clock in the hall, the creak of a floorboard, the faintest distant rumble of a train. Then – Boom! – there was a tremendous thud outside – and another – and another – getting louder, or nearer, or both. An extraordinary vibration rose up through the house, hit the soles of Alice's feet and went out through the top of her head. There was a sound nearby like the magnified swishing of a curtain. There was an immense cough.

Whereupon the giant baby spoke his first word: 'M A M A!'

How could he know, I wonder? For he had clearly known before the cough. Had he sensed his mother's presence, or recognized her motherly footsteps in the street? Who can tell? Well, *he* could tell, that was for sure, and shortly after yelled again.

'M A M A!'

At which point, a giant eye showed itself at the skylight, a giant handbag was set down in the garden and *the roof of the house* (like the lid of a teapot) –

> Judder!
> Creak!
> CRASH!
> – was lifted off.

Alice fell to her knees in shock. She saw the luminous sky above her head and heard her parents shouting:

'What's happening?'

'Help!'

And then a mightier voice, a gale-force voice, declared: 'M Y *L I T T L E* B A B Y!'

Alice staggered onto the landing. The baby was still there, but only just. A pair of giant hands (with polished fingernails and a couple of rings, Alice later recalled) were coming down.

'M A M A, M A M A!'

They grasped the baby, held him high . . . and carried
him away.

Alice gazed in horror and despair at the departing
baby. She would have rushed into the garden, but her
parents held her back. Meanwhile, there was that sound
again of a swishing curtain (a skirt, no doubt), followed
this time by a sort of zipping noise and a curious clink of
metal.

After which, one grateful giant mum: 'T H A N K Y O U! T H A N K Y O U A L L!', with one happy giant baby: 'M A M A!', moved off into the night.

ALICE AND HER PARENTS went down into the darkened hall. Swirls of plaster dust rose up around their feet. Bricks and lumps of plaster littered the stairs. A splintered rafter partly blocked the hall. Mr Hicks switched on the kitchen light and was surprised to find it worked. Alice scrambled out into the garden, with her mother close behind. Mr Hicks went looking for a torch.

The sky was black except for its luminous band of light. This light, this *aurora*, was brighter now. Flecks of orange and pink stood out against the green and white, the arc had dipped a little towards the horizon and periodically the whole expanse appeared to ripple like a flag in the wind.

Alice ignored this magical sight. She only cared for what she couldn't see: the giant baby. He was gone, disappeared completely and for ever, she could feel it. Tears welled up in her eyes and she began to sob.

Mrs Hicks put an arm around her. 'Don't cry, Alice. He's with his mother, after all.' She gave a sob herself. 'It's for the best – really, it is.'

'Maybe. It's not a happy ending, though, is it? No baby and hardly any house!'

Along the street, lights had been coming on in the neighbouring houses. Cautious figures in dressing-gowns and slippers had stepped out to investigate. Mr Hicks, torch in hand, joined his wife and daughter. He put his arms around them both and he cried, too.

'Oh, Dad!' sobbed Alice.

'Well, he's with his proper mother, I suppose.' Mr Hicks blinked his tears away.

'What gets me is,' said Alice, 'how she could ever have left him in the first place.'

'Who can say?' Mrs Hicks shrugged. 'Perhaps giant time is different from ours. Giant space is different.'

'Yes.' Mr Hicks took up the thread. 'She might only have put him down for a minute, as far as she thought. There again, maybe she was just forgetful –'

'You can't forget a baby!' cried Alice.

'No, I suppose not.' Mr Hicks left them and went down the side of the house. He was looking for the roof, having failed to notice it was out in the street. What he found, however, was something else.

'Hallo, what's this? Good grief! Marion – come quick!'

Alice and her mum rushed up.

'Where are you?'

'What's the matter?'

'Look!' Mr Hicks shone his torch on the ground to illuminate . . . a monstrous coin. It was bigger than a dustbin lid and thicker than a pile of books.

'What is it?' Alice cried.

'Gold!' yelled Mr Hicks. 'A ton of it – his mother's left a tip!'

17

A Little Prince

AND SO IT HAD COME to this for the giant baby: found on a doorstep, cared for by Alice and her parents, rented out by Horace, kidnapped by the Grubbling Brothers, rescued by Alice, nearly experimented on by Doctor Splitter, rescued again by a great many people, and reclaimed by his mum. For Alice, however, the list was shorter: she had wanted a baby brother, got one and lost him.

Alice, in the following days, was inconsolable. She went to school, but learnt nothing; ate her meals, but tasted not a thing. Her parents (the excitement of the gold soon passed) were in a similar state. The baby's departure had left a giant hole in all their lives. Fortunately there were distractions, things which had to be done or attended to; the wrecked house, for instance. The Hickses moved in temporarily with Auntie Joan and her family. Alice shared a room with Ethel. The police arrived in Tucker Street to investigate. They took away the rattle for forensic tests and discovered a bootee in the garden.

'Whosoever this bootee fits shall . . .' began Constable Dunkley, but Sergeant Fagg, the more sensitive of the two, frowned him into silence.

Despite a careful search, little evidence was found of the giant mother's trail. All the signs were that she had stepped delicately over fences and around parked cars. Legs like a rhinoceros she may have had, but at least she didn't charge about. So much for Professor Prewitt. One other thing: her lace hankie, the size of a sheet and embroidered with pink daisies, was found the following day in the next county; well, her alleged hankie, anyway.

THE DAYS AND, presently, the weeks went by. The rebuilding of the house began (and the rebuilding of the Hickses' lives). According to the small print in their insurance policy, Mr and Mrs Hicks were not covered for acts of God, or giants (or midgets, probably). Happily, the gold coin more than met the considerable cost of a new roof. There was even enough left over for an extra attic room, a modest garage and a second-hand, cardboard-box shaped Morris Oxford car.

By this time interest in the Hicks family had faded. Reporters ceased to call, the phone no longer rang incessantly, the post returned to its normal size. The pain of losing the giant baby had faded, too. Alice could bear to remember him now without distress. At Monica's birthday party she wore her favourite skirt and blouse, and had an (almost) marvellous time.

Meanwhile, the Grubbling *Family* Circus had departed to another town. Business continued to be brisk. The Underwater Sensations – a couple of Grubbling cousins in mermaid tails and a glass tank – returned to the fold. Basil's portrait was included in the latest set of Lloyd's cigarette cards (Fifty Famous Men). Queenie was considering a number of marriage proposals, one of which she eventually accepted.

On the subject of marriage, in the autumn – still hot and golden – the local reporter and his fiancée were married. Alice, to her delight, was invited to be a bridesmaid. By October the roof was back on the house and the Hickses back in it. Alice admired the new room and wondered aloud what it was for.

'Ironing!'

'Table tennis!' her parents said. And, 'Wait and see.'

In December Alice and her parents attended the first-night gala performance, in a London theatre, of: *Big Baby*, a musical play. Alice enjoyed the songs but was otherwise disappointed. Somehow it was just so . . . unconvincing. For one thing, the actor playing the baby was twenty-three years old and had a baby himself.

Christmas arrived. It turned out to be the hottest Christmas Day for four hundred years. (It was cooler in the Arizona desert.) Alice had ice-cream with her Christmas pudding – in the garden – in her swimming costume! Horace and his pals played cricket.

In the spring Professor Prewitt published a book entitled: *On Being the Wrong Size and Other Essays*. It contained a scientific explanation for the impossibility of giant babies. Apart from this, however, and a brief dance craze (The Dirty Bottom), the giant baby was by now forgotten. Other wonders took his place. A number of extremely *small* people had been sighted near Salford. There was a blue boy, by all accounts, in Denmark.

But Alice had not forgotten. Often, as she lay in bed, pictures of the giant baby flashed across her mind: the first time he had burped; the way he'd walloped Maurice with a pan; his high-speed crawling in the park; his chubby, thoughtful smile.

And then, one morning on a coolish day in June, Mr Hicks took Alice (and a bunch of flowers) to the Pear Street General Hospital, Ward Four (Maternity). Mrs Hicks was sitting up in bed in a brand-new bedjacket, with a brand-new baby in a cot beside her.

'Oh!' Alice peered into the cot. 'A little brother . . . of the proper size.'

'Six pounds, twelve ounces,' said her mum.

Mr Hicks was also peering. 'Is this him? My word, he looks like a –'

'Dad!' warned Alice.

But Mr Hicks well knew his part. 'Like a . . . little prince.' And he began to smile. 'Oh, yes – a baby and a half.'

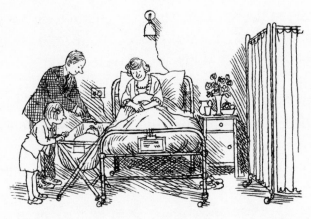

AR Ø